The Ski Mask Cartel 3

By T.J. Edwards

Lock Down Publications and
Ca$h Presents
Ski Mask Cartel 3
A Novel by *T.J. Edwards*

Lock Down Publications
P.O. Box 870494
Mesquite, Tx 75187

Visit our website
www.lockdownpublications.com

First Edition July 2018
Printed in the United States of America

Lock Down Publications
Like our page on Facebook: Lock Down Publications
@
www.facebook.com/lockdownpublications.ldp
Cover design and layout by: **Dynasty Cover Me**
Book interior design by: **Shawn Walker**
Edited by: **Lauren Burton**

Stay Connected with Us!

Text **LOCKDOWN** to 22828 to stay up-to-date with new releases, sneak peaks, contests and more…

Submission Guideline.

Submit the first three chapters of your completed manuscript to ldpsubmissions@gmail.com, subject line: Your book's title. The manuscript must be in a .doc file and sent as an attachment. Document should be in Times New Roman, double spaced and in size 12 font. Also, provide your synopsis and full contact information. If sending multiple submissions, they must each be in a separate email.

Have a story but no way to send it electronically? You can still submit to LDP/Ca$h Presents. Send in the first three chapters, written or typed, of your completed manuscript to:

LDP: Submissions Dept
Po Box 870494
Mesquite, Tx 75187

DO NOT send original manuscript. Must be a duplicate.

Provide your synopsis and a cover letter containing your full contact information.
Thanks for considering LDP and Ca$h Presents.

Dedications

This book is dedicated to my amazingly, beautiful stomp down wife, Mrs. Jelissa Shante Edwards, who knows firsthand what this Ski Mask life is all about. I've had to feed our family many nights using that to make it happen. But, for you, I had to find another way because you deserve the best, and my place to be is beside you, protecting you at all times. You're my motivating force that keeps me going. No matter how old you get, you'll always be *my* baby girl. So, deal with it. I love you forever and always. Your husband.

Acknowledgments

Shout out to Cash and Shawn. I love ya'll with all my heart... not only as a C.E.O and C.O.O, but as brother and sister. This is me and my wife's home. You already know that our loyalty is sealed in blood. Mad love to the entire LDP family.

Chapter 1

Rayjon pulled Kenosha to her feet roughly, yanking her up while one of his goons placed his hand around Madison's mouth. His other goon picked me up and kept his shotgun pointed at the back of my head. I felt sick. I felt trapped and couldn't believe I had allowed my family to be snatched up by my enemies in such a way. Every time I heard my daughter's mother yelp from the pain Rayjon was applying to her, it made me want to throw up and snap out at the same time, but I was in no position to do either one. I knew I had to use my head or all of us were about to be murdered.

We traveled through my dark house until we wound up downstairs in the basement. Rayjon and his goons sat my daughter Madison, her mother Kenosha, and myself on the floor and made us scoot all the way back until our backs were against the brick wall. Two goons stood in front of us. One had a shotgun pointed to my forehead while the other one had a Mossberg pump up against Kenosha's temple. Madison snuggled up under my armpit, shaking. Feeling her doing that literally broke my heart in half.

"I'm so scared, Daddy. I'm so, so scared," she whimpered and stuck her face further under me.

I looked to my right and saw tears rolling down Kenosha's cheeks, her eyes wide open looking at the ceiling of the basement. She swallowed hard, and then turned to look me in the face.

"Why are they doing this to us, Racine? We ain't did nothin' to them." Her teeth started to chatter, and I knew it wasn't from being cold. She was scared out of her mind and didn't know what was to become of us. The worst feeling a man could ever experience was not being able to protect those who were closest to him, especially when they were female.

Rayjon had been pacing back and forth as if in deep thought. When he heard those words come out of Kenosha's mouth, it caused him to stop in his tracks. I was about to respond to what Kenosha had asked, but he cut me off by clapping his hands together loudly. "Fuck, I got it. I know what I'ma do for you, even though I know yo' bitch-ass don't deserve it." He walked over to me and knelt down with an evil grin on his face. "Nigga, I'ma throw you a bone since I did kill yo' momma and shit." He laughed at that, and I wanted to jump up and choke this nigga to death, but once again I was in no position to.

Less than an hour ago I watched him viciously slay my mother in front of me. Rayjon was seeking his revenge because I had crossed him, along wit' his woman. After she took a liking to me, she'd helped me hit his safe house, and together we cleaned him out for every penny he had. That was over a million plus dollars, not including the bricks of heroin.

Along the way two of his li'l niggaz he'd brought down from Jersey were also bodied. One was killed by my cousin Tez, who was laid up in the hospital fighting for his life after catching a few slugz. Rayjon's wife Averie had bodied the other one. If it had been up to me, I would have hit up both niggaz, but I was laying on the pavement myself after inhaling a few bullets. It was all a part of the game, and now I was facing the consequences and had to find a way to get myself and my family out of this sticky situation. I had so many enemies gunning for me, but by far Rayjon was the deadliest.

He curled his upper lip. "Nigga, you gon' pay me three million in cash before May first. In addition to that, you gon' bring me Averie's head in a bag, along wit' yo' cousin's. And in exchange for all of that, I'm gon' let one of them live, and I'm gon' let you pick which one you gon' kill. It's gon' come down to who you love the most. Is it gon' be yo' daughter? Or is it gon' be yo' pregnant-ass baby mother? I'm giving you five minutes to take this offer and make that choice. The clock is ticking, my nigga. Tick tock." He cheesed and stood up, taking a few steps back and all the while looking me in the eyes with his lip curled up. "Hurry up!"

Kenosha started to shake right away with her eyes closed, shaking her head side-to-side. "No. No. No. Please don't make him make that decision. Don't do this to our family, Rayjon. I am begging you," she cried, her face now full of tears.

Rayjon smiled and looked down at his Rolex watch. "Tick tock, nigga. Three minutes now."

11

"Daddy, I'm scared," Madison whimpered again.

My head was spinning worse than a tornado. I felt sick as hell. What was I supposed to do? It was one of those decisions that were impossible to make. I loved Kenosha with all my heart. We had been together ever since we were little kids. Even back then, before we knew was love was, we knew we were in it. She had always been real stomp-down for me and held me down through some of the toughest of situations. I knew I could never kill her or watch her die. She was low-key my everything.

"Two minutes, nigga! Tick tock!" Rayjon hollered, and I could hear his goons snicker.

When it came to my daughter, Madison, I loved her first and foremost. She was my heart and soul. Before she was even born I made sure I hit them streets every single day to keep my pockets fat in preparation of her coming. Since she was born I made it my business to make sure she never needed or wanted for anything.

My daughter was my purpose for being alive. But then again, so was her mother.

I shook my head. "Rayjon, just kill me and get this over wit', man. They ain't got nothin' to do wit' none of this. This is between me and you. Kill me and let them go. Let's be men about this."

Rayjon looked at his Rolex. "Forty-five seconds, nigga. You betta make yo' mind up or I'ma make it up for you."

Kenosha opened and closed her eyes again, laying her head back against the brick wall. A trail of snot slid out of her nostrils and dripped down her thick lips. Tears sailed from her cheeks and landed on her blouse, saturating it.

"Ten seconds, Racine. I hope you know I ain't playin wit' you, my nigga." He frowned and took a Glock .40 out of the small of his back, still looking down at his watch. "Nine, eight, seven, six, five, four, three, two, one." He scrunched his face and walked over to Madison with his gun out, grabbin' her arm roughly in an attempt to pull her away from me.

She screamed and kicked her legs wildly. "Ah! Daddy! No! Ah!"

I held onto her arm and tried to pull her back down to me. "Nall, don't kill my daughter. Please, Rayjon. Not my baby girl, man." I pulled her into my arms and covered her entire body with that of my own.

Rayjon held her hand for a few seconds longer and then let it go. "If it ain't her, that mean it's her, then." He took a step from in front of me and Madison and looked down on Kenosha.

She kept her eyes closed. Tears continued to leak out of her eyelids, running down her cheeks and dripping from her chin.

"You hear that, Kenosha? This nigga choosing his daughter over you and y'all unborn kid. What type of nigga is he?" Rayjon laughed and then snatched her up by her neck real rough-like. "Open yo' fucking mouth, right now!" he spat into her face.

Kenosha opened her mouth wide, and as soon as she did Rayjon slid his Glock into it and damn-near forced it all the way down her throat before slamming her against the wall. She gagged on his weapon, kicked her legs, and tried to remove the gun to no avail.

"Racine, either you take yo' arms from around that li'l girl or I'm finna blast yo' baby momma. Because right now you telling me you choosing yo' daughter over yo' bitch. I'm counting to three, and shorty ass dead. Blood, if he take his arms from around that li'l girl, blow her head off ASAP." He ordered his masked goon, to which the goon pumped the shotgun and nodded his head. "What's it gon' be, Racine?"

I didn't want to think in that moment because I didn't know what to do. All I knew was I had to protect my daughter at all costs. It was my job. She wasn't nothin' but a li'l girl. She needed her father's protection. I would die for her in a heartbeat. At the same time, I needed to save Kenosha, but I knew I couldn't. In my heart I was making the decision to save Madison and let Kenosha eat Rayjon's bullets, but I just couldn't mentally submit to that fact. It would destroy me.

"Three. Two."

I held Madison more firmly and kissed my daughter's cheek as tears fell from my eyes. I couldn't believe I was about to lose Kenosha. I would never forgive myself. I didn't know how I was going to get Rayjon back. All I knew was one day real soon I would.

Kenosha squeezed her eyes tighter. "It's okay, Racine. Just protect her when I'm gone and know I will always love you."

Rayjon started to choke her with one hand. "Two. One!" He put the pistol to her head and pulled back the hammer.

I expected to hear the gun blast. I closed my eyes tight and awaited the sound of it, but nothin' came. Slowly I opened my eyes to see Rayjon looking into Kenosha's eyes with a mug on his face.

He laughed and shook his head. "As much as I hate you, Racine, I can't kill no pregnant woman. Especially when she didn't have shit to do wit' none of this. I'm a cold nigga, but not that cold." He threw her to the ground and walked over to me and Madison, grabbing a handful of her long hair and trying to yank her from my arms. "Nigga, let her go 'fore I put a bullet in her head!"

I opened my arms reluctantly and watched him pick my daughter up by her hair while she screamed and thrashed her limbs in the air. "Daddy! Daddy! Daddy! Help!" Her little arms reached out for me, and Rayjon's goon put his shotgun to my forehead, pressing it hard up against my skin. So hard a trickle of blood leaked out of the broken skin and trailed down my face. I was seconds away from making him pull that trigger when Rayjon started talking.

"Since I see you care about her the most, she gon' be a pawn in all of this. You gon' get me my money and them heads or I'm gon' cut yo' daughter apart piece-by-piece. You owe me three million dollars by May first. I expect my first payment of one million in two weeks. You late, and she losing an arm. Until I got my money and them heads, nigga, I own you. You gon' do what the fuck I say and how I say to do it. I got a list of licks I want you to hit, and every penny is to come back to me. It ain't got nothin' to do wit' my three million. Just consider that interest." He picked Madison up and held her on his hip while she cried and cried, still reaching out for me. "Get my money, Racine, and get them heads. I'd love to kill this pretty li'l girl. She won't cost me one wink of sleep." He snapped his fingers and his goon walked over to him, pulled out a roll of duct tape, took a bit of it, ripped it off, and placed it over Madison's mouth. After that was done, Rayjon started to walk to the stairs with her.

I wanted to jump up so bad, but the shotgun was still against my forehead, preventing me from doing so. "Rayjon, I'll do whatever you want, man. You ain't gotta take my daughter. Why we can't leave this shit between me and you?"

Rayjon looked over his shoulder while he held Madison and laughed. "Nigga, you made this bigger than me and you when you betrayed me wit' my bitch. After you kilt that loyalty, you made everybody and everything fair game. You did this shit. The bed is made, now lie in it." He looked at his goons. "Keep that nigga at bay until you hear my truck drive off. He move, knock a chunk out of his baby momma. I ain't playin', either."

The last time I saw my daughter, she was reaching out for me and crying, her pretty face red. Her screams were muffled because of the tape, but I could still hear them. They were loud enough to kill my soul.

Five minutes later I heard the sounds of Rayjon's tires screechin' away from the curb. I saw one goon slam the handle of his Mossberg into the back of Kenosha's head before she fell to her stomach, knocked out cold, then the other one knocked me out the same way. My last thoughts were of my daughter's red face screaming out for me.

T.J. EDWARDS

Chapter 2

As crazy as it may sound, me and Kenosha stayed cooped up in the house for the next four days, trying our best to mentally pick up the broken pieces of our lives. I was so lost, and I could not stop breaking down. The police found my mother the next morning after her murder. How? I didn't know, but what I did know was my grandmother identified her body, and her funeral was set for the following Wednesday. I had already made up my mind I wasn't going, and I wasn't intending on talking to no police about it. I knew what had to be done. This was street bitness, and that's where I intended to keep it. Though I was sick over her murder, the longing for my daughter prevented me from grieving the way I guess I was supposed to.

On the fourth day of us being in the house, I had been lying in the bed with my eyes closed, unable to sleep when Kenosha left the kitchen, came into our bedroom, and slammed the door so hard it caused me to sit upright in the bed after pulling my .9 mm from under the pillow and cocking it back, ready to blast somethin'.

She looked into my face with flared nostrils. "Racine! I'm sick and tired of you just lying around while our daughter is out there with her life on the line, probably crying her little heart out waiting for her daddy to rescue her from them damn demons. But here you are, lying around the house like a fucking pussy. Nigga, get yo' ass up and go get my baby!" She scrunched her face and looked like she was ready to put her hands on me.

I felt so sick and weak. I had not eaten since I'd lost my daughter, so I was dizzy. On top of that, my heart was heavy. I didn't have the energy or the strength to fight wit' her.

I stood up and turned my back to her, getting ready to slide my pistol back under the pillow when she grabbed my shoulder and made me face her. "What the fuck is you gon' do, Racine? Huh? You finna let this nigga take our baby away? You just gon' sit back and let him punk us like this? Huh?" She blinked tears. "I ain't never known for you to be so fuckin' weak. So soft." She curled her upper lip.

I turned back around and tossed my gun on the bed before sitting right beside it. I took my hands and rubbed them over my face with my eyes closed. I was so dizzy. I was trying to make sense of things.

I felt Kenosha get close to me. That caused me to open my eyes, and that's when I was met with her holding my gun in my face with tears streaming down her cheeks. She pulled back the hammer.

"You chose her over me, Racine. You chose for me to die and for her to live, and that shit killed me, Racine." She sniffed snot back into her nostrils. "Now they took her and you ain't doing shit about it. What kind of man are you?"

I hopped up and put my forehead on the barrel of the gun with tears running down my cheeks. I held it with both hands. "Well, kill me then,

Kenosha, because I can't take this shit! That bitch-ass nigga got my daughter! I failed to protect her, and that shit is eating away my soul. I'm lost. Kill me. Fuck this life, anyway!" I hollered, feeling myself shaking like crazy. I missed Madison so bad I didn't know what to do. I wished Kenosha had pulled that trigger. Things would have been so much easier for me, as pussy as that may have sounded.

She dropped the gun and wrapped her arms around me, crying into my chest. "No, baby. I could never hurt you. You already know that. I just want you to go out there and fight like you're supposed to for our family. Go make it happen. My whole life I ain't had to depend on nobody but you because you always come through. Now I know you're hurting, and I know you're down right now, but this family needs you more than ever." She grabbed my chin with her hand and held it firm, looking into my eyes. "That nigga has our daughter. Our little baby. You gon' let him do us like that? Huh?" She raised her right eyebrow.

I swallowed as I looked into her eyes, and the look she gave me just made me snap out of it. I went from tears running out of my eyes to frowning with hatred beating in my heart. There was no way I was finna let this nigga out-think me or get away with killing my mother and taking my daughter away from me.

I was a street savage. Chicago was my homeland, and the worst thing an out-of-town nigga could ever do was try to oppose me on my stomping grounds. I had to murder Rayjon and master the game.

I stood up and wiped my face with my chest heaving up and down. "I'm fuckin' up, Kenosha. I mean I fucked up, but I'm finna get shit back right. I promise." I took a deep breath and blew it back out slowly. "I'm finna get our daughter back, and I'ma kill this nigga. Don't nobody mess wit' my girls. I'll do anything for y'all. I got this, baby. Just you watch."

She nodded and walked into my face. "That's my nigga, right there. You don't bow down to nobody. We'll all die together before we let this nigga punk us. Go out there and make it happen."

Twenty minutes later I was jumping out of the shower and Kenosha was shoving a plate of her homemade French toast and scrambled cheese eggs in my face. At the first sight of it I almost puked because I was still sick over my mother and Madison, but I knew I had to eat to get my strength up, so I banged that shit and drunk me a bottle of chocolate Ensure she kept in our refrigerator.

E pulled up to my crib about ten minutes later, rolling a black Navigator. I jumped into the passenger's seat and noted Wayne was in one of the back seats with an all-black Uzi on his lap with a long-ass clip sticking out of it.

"Man, I don't know who dis Rayjon nigga is, but I'm down to knock his head off for you, big homie. I went to yo' mom's funeral out of respect for you and saw the way he did her." He lowered his head and shook it. "Now he got yo' daughter.

Just tell me what to do?" Wayne said, sucking on his gold teeth.

He was one of my li'l niggaz that ate in the slums. Li'l homie was from the gutter, just like me and my cousin Tez, and I had much love and respect for him and that nigga E. "Yo, I appreciate you sayin' that, li'l homie, and I already know you fuckin' wit' me on that level. I'm putting things together, and you gon' know how to move as soon as I figure it out."

He pulled away from the curb, puffing on a blunt. "Big homie, you already know what it is wit' me. I'm willing to wet that nigga whole bloodline, including his moms if it come down to that. You and yo' cousin the only niggaz out here that's making sure me, and my people eat, so for that alone I pledge my loyalty to you in blood." He scrunched his fat, yellow face and nodded.

The homie E was pure savage, just like Wayne. It was a reason I kept both killas close to my chest. It was because I trusted their gangsta.

"I appreciate those words, E. You already know how shit finna go down." I looked over my shoulder at Wayne as he slammed the clip back into the Uzi, sat it on his lap, then fixed the leather gloves on his hands. "How my cousin doing?"

Wayne looked up at me. "He doing better. He out of the intensive care unit and in a regular hospital bed. He talking and everything. He say them people been all over him, but Ellie been holdin' him down in that department, so that's what's up."

I nodded my head. I loved my cousin, and it kilt me to watch him get hit up with them slugs like that. I knew it was a part of the game, but it still stunk.

Ellie was a li'l chick I had met at the club a few weeks back. She was Puerto Rican, bad, and was a part of the Cook County Police Academy. She was a few weeks away from becoming a full-fledged police officer. I was trying to figure out a way to use that to my advantage because she secretly hated cops after they gunned down her brother in cold blood.

"I know before we jump into anything we gotta take a good look at these BDs over here on 69th. I was riding wit' my daughter two days ago and they shot my car up. I was lucky none of them bullets went through the body and hit my baby girl. It's buzzing through the land that we had somethin' to do wit' J-Rock getting kilt. Muthafuckas just speculatin', but in the hood that's all it take." He cocked the Uzi. "I ain't taking that shit lying down, so let's hit they ass up. Then we can get on this other shit."

E nodded. "Yeah, bruh, they having some picnic outside right now at Gage Park. We gotta splash them niggaz and make a statement or muthafuckas finna come at the Taylors before we even start to get the kind of money we know we gon' be getting. Anytime one crew fall in Chicago, it's always a hunnit other ones that's looking to take over they turf."

"Yeah, and muthafuckas out here real hungry, too. I'm talking starving, especially when it come down to owning the Taylors. That muthafucka can gross over five hunnit thousand a day, so you already know what it is. J-Rock was plugged wit' these BDs that we finna hit up. The reason we gotta make a splash is because since they were so close to him, they feel like they should be next in line to move into the Taylors. They must've heard about who Denzell standing behind, and that shit got them heated, which is why they took a few shots at my whip," Wayne said, reaching under his seat and handing me a Mach .90 wit' an eighty-round clip.

I took it and pulled the clip out, looked it over and noted it was filled to the max, then popped it back into the Mach and cocked it. My heart was killing me over missing my daughter. I felt like I needed to kill somethin' just to take my mind off her for a minute or two. In all honesty, I knew this was a detour and going in the opposite direction of where I should have been going to get my daughter back, but in Chicago it was all about honoring and riding wit' the niggaz who would put they lives on the line for you. On top of that, Wayne and E both made valid points. If we didn't go right at the niggaz that had shot up Wayne's whip, they would think we were sweet and come at the Robert Taylor Home Projects we had stripped away from J-Rock and his crew.

Wayne had also spoken about Denzell. Denzell was a powerful alderman who was pulling strings to help ensure we were able to push our product all throughout his ward and district with very little resistance from the local authorities. In exchange for his pull, we were to pay him a certain amount of paper every week and bust a few moves in his rival's district – a rival he no longer had because we had taken care of him only a few weeks back.

E handed me a white ski mask as he made a left onto Jackson Drive where Gage Park was located. He slowed his speed and slipped a white ski mask over his face as well. Behind us, Wayne did the same thing.

"Look, bruh, after we handle this bitness right here, we gotta get on this mission to get my daughter back. Money will be the focal point by any and every means. Y'all got that?" I asked, looking from one to the next.

Wayne sucked his teeth. "Nigga, you already know. Just tell me what to do and that shit done. I'm riding for you, big homie, in a bloody way."

E nodded. "I got you. You lead, and I'll follow."

He slowly turned onto the block where Gage Park started. As soon as we bent the corner, I saw the street was lined with all types of foreign cars. People had their car doors open, sitting inside and just letting their music blast. Most had females on the side of the whips dancing or twerking, depending on the song being played. The sun was still out and shining bright. It felt like it had to be about sixty degrees out, early spring.

As we slowly turned onto the block, I also noted to our left were a bunch of people already at the park with picnic tables scrunched together and about six barbecue grills going. To the right of the grills were about fifty dudes with blue t-shirts on and the brims of their fitted caps turned to the right to symbolize they rolled under the Black Disciples.

In Chicago anyone could identify what side a gang rolled with by the way they tilted the brims of their fitted caps. Tilted to the left meant they ran under gangs under the five-point star. The left usually meant either red and black or gold and black. Tilted to the right meant they rode under the six-point star or were a close affiliate or ally of all gangs under the six. Their colors usually were blue and black, or green and black for the Mexican gangs under the six.

As we rolled up, I saw all these dudes dressed in blue and black with their hats tilted to the right. Even though E and Wayne rolled wit' gangs under the same colors and star, they didn't give a fuck because wit' us, it was all about money and loyalty between one another over everythang else.

E slowly cruised down the street, allowing us to take in the scenery. I kept my eyes on the park. I was trying to figure out how we were going to hit up as many of them as possible without hitting the kids who were peppered around them here and there. I didn't give a fuck about killing no grown-ass niggaz, but I wasn't wit' killing no kids. Females neither, unless I absolutely had to.

"E, on some real shit, I think we gon' have to do what we said we was last night, even though I know you probably don't wanna go that route. I'm trying to kill up these niggaz. They could've hit my baby wit' one of them bullets, nigga," Wayne said, looking out of his window with his hand on his Uzi. He had a mug on his face that said he hated the niggaz we was looking at.

E shrugged his shoulders. "Fuck it. I'm cool wit' it long as you is, Racine." He looked over to me and turned right, headed down a one-way street before making another right on his way back toward the park.

I frowned. "Is what okay wit' me? What y'all have in mind? 'Cuz I don't see how we finna hit all these niggaz up and miss these kids that's out there."

E frowned his chubby face. "We finna jump that curb and head right for them niggaz. Ain't no other way. Y'all just gotta be ready to shoot, 'cuz they most definitely is. I'm gon' come through the back way right from around the basketball courts, that way we'll get as close as possible to that crowd and can chop they asses down. Then I can head down the one-way and roll five blocks before we back on the expressway and up out this area. Me and Wayne'll chop they ass down again in the middle of the night tonight just to let them know they don't want these kind of problems. We got a few li'l niggaz that's fuckin' wit' us we gon' introduce you to later. Some certified li'l head-bustahs that's already screaming cartel life."

I took a deep breath and exhaled slowly. I just wanted to get this shit over wit'. The faster we got it over and done wit', the faster I could get on this bitness of getting my daughter back from Rayjon. "Nigga, let's do it."

Less than two minutes later we were rolling back down the block the same way we had come the first time. The park had filled up a little more, and there were even more kids around, sitting at the picnic tables eating or throwing around a football while the girls jumped double-dutch in the parking lot a little away from the crowd of savages we were targeting.

"Bruh, y'all try to miss them li'l girls right there. They ain't got shit to do wit' this," I said, thinking about Madison. I missed her with my entire being.

Wayne sucked his gold teeth again loudly. "Man, bullets ain't got no names on 'em, big homie. They betta get they ass out the way when I start busting, because I'm looking to kill everythang. Didn't no muthafucka take my daughter's life into consideration when they was airing me out the other day. So fuck all that. Let's handle this bitness," he retorted, lowering his mask.

I wanted to say somethin' real slick to 'em, but I decided to keep my comments to myself. The worst thing to ever do when you was going on a move to kill somebody was to beef wit' the niggaz you was pullin' the lick wit. You never knew when the murdering would drive a nigga crazy, and the next thing you'd know his gun could be aiming at you. Chicago was fucked up, full of niggaz like me who didn't give a fuck about killing another man. The hood had instilled this sense of no remorse in us every since we were little kids.

He pulled the Navigator into the parking lot and drove it way to the back of it before hitting a U-turn and facing where the group of BDs were gathered. They looked to be about sixty deep now, huddled around, laughing and joking, oblivious to the fact they were about to be attacked.

"Y'all ready?" E asked, lowering his window and sitting his AK47 on his lap.

I nodded and grabbed my Mach .90. "Let's do this shit, li'l bruh."

Wayne grunted. "Punch that gas and hit a few of they ass. That'll make shit even easier."

E nodded, rolled his head around on his shoulders as he mugged the group off in the distance, then slammed his foot on the gas.

Chapter 3

Vroom! The truck took off like a rocket, and I was surprised at how close we were able to get before any of the niggaz in the groups spotted us coming at them, but it had been too late. We were no longer rolling on concrete, but the grass they were standing on. They began to scatter like roaches when the lights came on. I sat on the window with my Mach going nuts. *Thot-thot-thot! Thot-thot-thot! Thot-thot-thot! Thot-thot-thot!*

Wayne was behind me, leaning out of his window and making his Uzi bark. *Bop-bop-bop-bop-bop-bop-bop-bop!*

I saw our bullets flying into niggaz's chests and creating big holes that spewed blood. They would jerk backward and twist to their sides before shaking on the grass. Others tried to run and were hit up in the back, big holes filled them before they fell forward and landed on their faces, bleeding profusely. Little kids started to scream before running toward the playground while other dropped to the ground and covered their heads while me and Wayne kept letting our guns bark. *Thot-thot-thot! Bop-bop-bop! Thot-thot-thot!*

Boom! Boom! Boom! Our windshield shattered and caved in. Glass fell on my lap and even popped in my face as more bullets flew in our direction. *Boom! Boom! Boom! Boom!*

"E, step on the gas, nigga. They busting behind us!" Wayne hollered, ducking down in his seat and fitting a new clip into his Uzi. E stepped on the gas and Wayne fell to the floor, then came up busting out of the back window that had also shattered from our enemy's bullets.

Bop-bop-bop-bop-bop-bop! "Bitch-ass niggaz!" *Bop-bop-bop-bop-bop-bop!*

I stuck my head out the window and saw there was about four niggaz ducked behind an Escalade, busting at us wit' handguns while the girls who had been in the parking lot jumping rope lay on the pavement with their hands over their heads.

Boom! Boom! Boom! Boom! They kept on shooting.

I let loose in their direction, even opening my door a li'l bit so I could get a better shot at them. I had a tough time holding the Mach .90 steady wit' my left hand. I was cool when I was busting at the targets in front of me because I could use my right hand to aim, but since I had to bust at the fuck-niggaz behind, I had to reposition myself and use my left hand being that I was sitting in the passenger's seat.

E smashed into a few picnic tables and knocked over a barbecue grill full of steaks before driving across the grass and hitting a U-turn, heading back for the parking lot because it was the only way to exit the park, but now it seemed like the BDs had tripled in size and weapons. Before we could even make it back to the parking lot they let our ass have it with so many bullets the truck felt like it was finna fall over.

Boom! Boom! Boom! Boom! Boo-wa! Boo-wa! Boo-wa! Boo-wa! Tat-tat-tat-tat-tat-tat! Boom! Boom! Boom! Boom! Sssssssss! One of the tires was hit, causing it to become flat. The truck now wobbled as it rolled. Soon as we hit the pavement of the parking lot, the shots got worst. All our windows were shattered, and we were basically driving a death trap. So many bullets came that it was impossible to get up and bust back because they were coming that fast. The truck was smoking, and I don't know how E did it, but he kept that bitch rolling right on past them and to the streets, where he crashed into a van that was driving down the block. *Wham!* The impact threw me forward in my seat and activated the air bags. E landed up against me with blood coming from his forehead.

"Fuck that! Let's get out and run, come on. Here these niggaz come!" Wayne hollered and opened the back door, jumping out. *Bop-bop-bop-bop-bop-bop-bop!* Then he took off running.

Before I could even open my door, two big bullets slammed into it so hard it rocked the truck. I still opened it and took off running wit' E right behind me. I was scared out of my mind, and them niggaz kept on busting like they wanted our heads knocked off.

Wayne was so slim and so fast he was way out front and putting more distance in between me and E, but we was booking it. When we got to the next block, I decided to split up from them, so I took an alley and started running right back toward where we had come from. I figured them niggaz would have never thought nobody would have done that.

E and Wayne took off across the busy street as I jumped a fence and ran behind somebody's house with my heart pounding in my chest. I could barely breathe. I heard more gunshots ring. I looked behind me and didn't see nobody chasing me, so I figure they were on E and Wayne's asses. E's more so because he was running slow as hell.

I ran up to the back door, kicked it in with one kick, and fell onto the steps inside of the house before jumping up and closin' the door. Then I ran into the house.

As I was running into it, an old man was walking into his kitchen, nearly crashing into me. I raised my Mach immediately. "Look, sir, I don't want to hurt you, but it's somebody out there trying to kill me. I can't leave yo' house until they leave. Can I use yo' phone?"

The old man was holding a plate in his hand that had chicken bones and hot sauce residue. He scrunched his face at me and walked past me. "What's wrong wit' you young boys always trying to kill each other when it's the white man that's killing us all?" he said, setting the plate in the sink.

I bucked my eyes. I couldn't believe me being in his house with a mask on my face and a gun in my hand didn't phase him one bit. "Excuse me?"

He walked past me again, almost bumping me out of the way. "Look, the phone is over there. Call whoever you need to call to get you out of this mess, but you meet them down the street. I don't want my house being targeted for somethin' you did. Lord knows Jesus got a better plan for you than this." He waved me off and walked back to the living room.

I didn't even follow him. I grabbed up the phone with my gloves still on my hands and called a yellow cab. I knew that was the only way I was gon' get out of the area, but before the company even answered the phone I thought about me having to take my mask off to get inside the cab and knew it would be a no-go. My only hope was Ellie, so I called her and told her I needed her to meet me down the block ASAP. She said she would be there in ten minutes.

Right after I called her I called the Chicago Police Department and told them there were three people shot four houses down and the house was also on fire, then I hung up the phone. I knew from just living in Chicago that whenever the police were called about a stabbing or shooting or anything of the like they always sent the fire department first, then the paramedics before they showed up. I was trying to get that block filled up with sirens and as many people as possible before I stepped back out there into that death zone. I didn't think them niggaz was crazy enough to bust a move on me with the police and fire trucks present.

I waited for ten minutes, then walked into the living room where the old man was sitting, watching an old rerun of *Sanford and Son*. His living room was cluttered with all kinds of old stuff. It smelt funny, and there was barely any room to walk. When I stepped into it, he looked up at me with a slight mug on his face.

"Uh, excuse me, suh, but do you have a hoodie or something I can leave out of here wit'? My ride gon' meet me down the street, but of course I can't go out looking like this."

Just as I said that, I heard a bunch of sirens and horns from the fire trucks blaring loudly.

He waved me off again and pointed to a coat rack full of all kinds of coats. I jogged over to it and started to go through them one-by-one until I found an army fatigue hoodie. I slipped it across my back, put the hood on my head, and pulled on the strings on the side of it before I hit it out of his back door and down the alley at full speed.

I ain't gon' lie and say I wasn't paranoid, because I was. As I got to the middle of the alley I heard the fire engines turn onto the street, followed by the police. As soon as that happened, it seemed like niggaz started running from out of everywhere. They flew into the alley, then ran onto the next block wit' guns in their hands, running from the block that had all of the local authorities on it. I kept right on running wit' my heart beating faster and faster.

God must've been on my side because as I was coming out of the alley, Ellie was pulling up to the corner. I ran up to her passenger door and knocked on the glass. She jumped and pointed a .9 millimeter at me with her eyes wide. I shook my head and took my mask off, pulling back my hoodie just enough to reveal myself. Only then did she pop the lock, and I jumped in as she sped away from the curb.

I slumped down in the seat and pulled on the strings of my hoodie. "Damn, you showed up just in time. These niggaz over here don't play no games. Fuck."

She shook her head, then looked over at me while at the same time making sure she paid attention to the traffic that was in front of our car. "You know, ever since I met you it ain't been nothin' but trouble circling around you? Now what have you gotten your self into, *Papi*?"

I slid lower in my seat as two police cars sped past us and headed in the direction I had just come from. I didn't know if they were going to the block I called them to or the park where me and my homies left a bunch leaking.

"What you talkin' 'bout, Ellie?"

She laughed. "You betta be lucky I like bad boys or else I would arrest yo' ass, nigga, and take you in for whatever reward they probably got out for you. Nall, I got a better one. I would trade you in to graduate from the academy earlier instead of going through all the extra bullshit they trying to take me through." She licked her lips and made a left onto the expressway.

As we got further on, I sat upright in my seat. "Alright now, you know I don't know you well enough to play like that. I'll have to bust yo' head to make sure you can't do none of that shit that you talkin' about." I was smiling, but I was kind of serious because I was involved in way too much shit. I was sure we had killed at least fifteen people. I mean, I might have been overestimating by a few people, but I was sure I wasn't. Later on that night, the news confirmed that I had underestimated the number. There were twenty-five people shot, and eighteen had been killed. I could only vouch for bodying about seven of them.

Ellie poked out her lip and looked at me as if she were a little girl. "Damn, *Papi*, you would bust my head like that, for real? I thought you were starting to care about me a little bit." She looked over at me, made a sad face, then stared back out the window. "You know I would never turn you in. I got more gangsta in me than you think. Don't get it twisted because I'm going through the academy. I already told you I'm on somethin' in honor of my brother."

I lowered my window a li'l bit, so I could get some fresh air. Madison crept into my mind, and I was starting to feel sick all over again. I had to figure out how I was going to get my baby back. I also needed to know if Wayne and E were okay. Last I saw they had a gang of niggaz on they ass wit' pistols busting. I was a little worried about them.

I noticed Ellie had been a li'l quiet for about two minutes straight, and that made me snap out of my zone. The sun was starting to set, bringing on the night. "Say, look, Ellie, I was just playin' wit' you. I'd never do nothin' to you. I appreciate everything you've done for me and my cousin because you ain't have to do none of it. I know you got that gangsta shit in you in more ways than one, so I ain't questioning that for a second, trust me." I reached over and rubbed her chin, and then her soft cheek.

Her frown slowly turned into a smile, showing off a dimple almost as deep as the ones I had on my cheeks when I smiled. "I'm saying you betta put some respect on my gangsta." She laughed and flipped her long curly hair over her right shoulder, then tucked a li'l bit of it behind her right ear, looking over at me and sucking on her bottom lip.

Her mannerisms were driving me crazy, I ain't even gon' lie. To me there was nothing like a sexy female. I had to shake my head to snap out of the zone she was placing me in. "Say, where are you taking me?"

She gave me a devilish look, making her shoulder rise to her chin a li'l bit. "Aw, so what? You don't trust me now?"

I shook my head. "It ain't that I don't trust you, I just got so much shit I gotta take care of. I wish I could just chill wit' you, but right now ain't the time. Every second that passes could cost somebody that's real close to me their life."

She swallowed and bugged her eyes out of her head. "Are you serious? Tell me who and I'll do the best I can to help you, I swear." She swallowed again and kept looking from the road back to me with a worried expression on her face.

I lowered my head and shook it. "I can't right now. I got you involved in way too much shit as it is. Just drop me off at my crib and I'll figure shit out on my own."

She scrunched her face. "Didn't you just lose your mother to murder not even three weeks ago? Huh?"

All I could do was keep my face pointed toward my lap. A big lump formed in my throat as I thought about my mother and how Rayjon had did her. Even though I didn't like hurting females, I knew without a shadow of a doubt I would kill his mother or any female close to him with no hesitation. I would never be able to forget how he did my mother. Never. "Yeah, I lost her. What's yo' point, Ellie?"

"My point, *Papi*, is that you don't have it all figured out. You're steady trying to do everything on yo' own, and all you're doing is watching more and more people get hurt. Eventually you're going to be next. Then what? Will you accept some help then, huh? Or will it be too late?" She rolled her eyes and kept on driving.

No matter what she said, I just didn't feel right telling her everything going on wit' me. Even though she had saved my ass a few times now, I still didn't trust her like that because I barely knew her, and I was involved in some heavy stuff. So, since I didn't know what to say to her, I just sat back and eyed her from the corner of my eye as she drove.

All the while I was missing my daughter and trying to get my mind right as best as I could. I had to get a million dollars to Rayjon as soon as possible. That wouldn't be the problem because I had more than that stashed away after hitting him for over a mill. The problem would come after I gave that bread up. Then I would be damn near broke, and he expected me to have another mill to him within the next two weeks. I didn't know how I was gon' come up wit' that kind of paper, then hit Denzell and feed my niggaz grinding in the Robert Taylor Home Projects wit' me. I had so many dilemmas I felt like I was about to go crazy.

I was so deep in my head that I didn't even realize Ellie had skipped my exit, and we wound up pulling in front of a brownstone on Pine and Vanburen. That was Latin Kings turf. Latin Kings ran under the five-point star and were loony as a muthafucka. They didn't like nothin' that didn't ride wit' their set, and they would kill yo' ass dead in a heartbeat. They were one of the deadliest gangs in the city of Chicago and abroad.

When she parked the car and turned off the ignition, I looked around outside and saw so many niggaz dressed in gold and black with their hats tilted to the left that I thought she was setting me up. My stomach started to turn, and I was trying to guess how many bullets I had left in my Mach. I knew it couldn't be nearly enough to handle the hunnit-plus dudes I was looking at. Straight ahead of our car and about half a block down was a train going past on the railroad tracks.

I frowned at Ellie. "Why you got me over here around all these damn Kings?" I asked, trying to figure out how I was finna get myself out of this situation and off the west side of town where I was out of bounds. I say out of bounds because if a nigga wasn't plugged wit' one of the mobs out west, he was basically fish food. The niggaz on the west side killed for no reason other than for their gang supremacy. They were serious, and I didn't fuck around out there.

Ellie smiled her dimpled smile. "Chill out. You're good 'cause you wit' me. My brother was an Inka over here. Even though he's gone, his juice still reigns supreme. Come on inside. I got a surprise for you."

As she said this she opened her car door, causing the interior lights to come on in the car. As the lights illuminated me, I saw the niggaz standing in front of the brownstone next to the one we were in front of started to walk toward the car wit' their hands under their shirts. I gripped my Mach and prayed I didn't have to blast somebody.

The group walked up to Ellie and I saw her talking to them, then she stood to the side and two of the twenty niggaz walked to my passenger door and yanked it open.

Chapter 4

I would have fell on my face if I hadn't caught my balance and jumped backward toward the driver's seat. I was sure it was a hit. I had let a broad set me up to be murdered, and it was nothin' I could do about it but empty my clip and inhale whatever they was finna spit at me.

"Say, *vato*, what you doing over here, homes? This King hood, nigga. Who you repping?" said a short Mexican dude with two teardrops under his left eye. Behind him his army upped their weapons and walked closer to the car.

My heart got to thumping in my chest. I had visions of sliding over to the driver's seat and bolting out that door, but I didn't know nothin' about the west side of Chicago other than the kats over there were super gangbangers. I tightened my grip on my Mach and got ready to up it at them and squeeze the trigger. I think the only reason I was hesitating was because I didn't know how many bullets I had left. I didn't think it was more than fifteen, though.

Ellie tried to run over to the car but was snatched up by one of the bandits. She kicked her legs in the air and twisted wildly in his grasp. "Let me down, Javier. You guys need to leave him alone. He's over here wit' me!" she hollered, kicking her legs.

"Take her over there, homes! Now!" the short Mexican with the teardrops shouted, pointing toward their brownstone. Then he turned back to me. "What you repping, *vato*? I ain't gon' ask you again."

I noted his boys stepping closer. Most of them started to cock their weapons, mugging the shit out of me as if they hated my guts already. My mind was nearly made up. I was finna start busting. I got to feeling like these niggaz was finna smoke me anyway. I put the Mach on my lap, so the short Mexican could see it. I knew I was probably committing suicide, but I didn't give a fuck. I wasn't about to let them ho me under no circumstances.

"I'm Ski Mask Cartel, nigga, and we ain't got no beef wit' y'all out here on the west side. We ain't red or blue, nor six nor five. We all about money. That's it. Ellie is my girl, and I got a lot of respect for her."

The short Mexican scrunched his face and looked over his shoulder at his crew. "You *vatos* ever hear about a click called the Ski Mask Cartel, homes? This *vato* say that's what he rep, and they not under the five or the six."

He crew got to shaking their heads, and the expressions on their faces said they were just as confused.

Javier stepped back over to the car after setting Ellie down in front of the brownstone they had been standing in front of when we pulled up. "Tell him to take his shirt off, homes. See if he's tagged. That will tell us everything." He took a .9 mm out of his waistband and cocked it. "Better hope you ain't got no six-point stars on you, *vato*. Cuz if so, *pow*! Straight in the head, homes." He curled his upper lip and looked me in the eye, evil-like.

I knew I ain't like these niggaz. I was gon' make sure if I got out of this situation, I was gon' kill up as many Kings as I could. I felt like they were trying to treat me like a bitch, but then my common sense kicked in. Almost every gang in Chicago followed the same procedure if they caught a nigga out of bounds. That is if they didn't pop him right away from them just thinking he was an enemy. They would strip him down to read his tats. Lucky for me, I had never gotten any. I didn't like following another man, so I wasn't plugged wit' no particular gang in Chicago. I was what I said I was, a Ski Mask Cartel solider.

"Take yo' shirt off, homes, and hurry up." Before I could even react quick enough, he reached and snatched the Mach off my lap and threw it to the ground. "That ain't enough fire power for us. Trust me, *vato*."

I mugged him for a long time, then shook my head. "A'ight, fuck it. Look, bruh." I took my shirt off and threw it on the driver's seat, then felt the short Mexican dude grab my wrist until I was out of the car. He turned me all the way around until my head was lying on the roof of it outside. Then this muthafucka had the nerve to go over my whole upper body wit' a flashlight. I felt humiliated and pissed the fuck off. I hated these niggaz.

After he finished checking me, he nodded his head. "*Órale, vato.* He's clean, homes. Put your pistols away." He looked into my eyes and scrunched his face. "I don't care who you're over here to see, homes. You check in with the Kings before you turn into our hood. We live and die for this turf. The blood of our brothas has been shed defending it, so we take this shit very serious. You get that?"

He gave me wild eyes and flared his nostrils as if he was mentally geeking himself up for me to give him a bogus response, but I wasn't stupid. I knew when I was outnumbered and outgunned. I nodded. "That's my bad, bruh. Like I said before, I don't know nothin' about this hood, but I do now."

"Yeah, you bet yo' ass you do." He looked over his shoulder and snapped his finger at Ellie while his crew continued to mug me with hatred in their eyes. She jogged over to him and stood before him.

"Yes, Jose?"

He put his hands on both of her shoulders and looked into her pretty face. "Ellie, *mi hermana.* You know the rules. It's wartime. We can't be having all sorts of *rivales* or oppositions in our hood. You know you have to get permission for that." He stroked her long, curly hair and smiled.

She lowered her head. "*Lo siento,* Jose. I'm sorry, but he's not against you guys. He's just spending some time with me. Is that alright?"

He held her small face in both of his hands and smiled. "How can I say no to you?" He looked down at his watch. "It's eight o'clock right now. He has until midnight to be out of King territory. If he's late, we will kill him." He kissed her on the cheek and circled his finger through the air, walking off with his crew behind him. A majority still looked over their shoulders at me with a mug on their faces.

I swear I hated them niggaz, but I took a fascination with how they got down. They were so structured and disciplined. They carried on how a cartel or a mob was supposed to, and I knew my crew needed that kind of structure.

A few moments later I followed Ellie into her building in silence. We got all the way to the top of the stairs when she turned around and faced me. "Look, I'm sorry, Racine. Please don't be mad at me. It's just how they are around here. My brother raised all of them to be like him. Are you angry?"

I shrugged my shoulders. I didn't want to get into all of that. I didn't know why she'd brought me all the way over to her crib, and I just wanted to find out and get up out of there, so I could get on my own bitness. I felt like I owed her the benefit of the doubt since she did so much for me and Tez already. "Nall, I'm good, Ellie. Let's just get on wit' everything. Show me why you brought me all the way over here."

She took her key out of her pocket and was about to put it into the lock when she turned around to face me again. "If you're not mad, why don't you kiss my lips and prove it to me?" She took another step forward until her nose was up against my own.

Her perfume drifted up my nostrils, intoxicating me. She smelled different, a little exotic. I wanted to get on wit' things, but at the same time kiss them pretty lips, so I did. I kissed them, then sucked them into my mouth, licked them, and sucked all over them again while she moaned into my face and pressed her crotch up against mine, making my dick become harder than I wanted it to at that time.

"Mm. Racine. Mm, baby," she moaned and ground harder into me, taking her hands and rubbing all up and down my back.

As crazy as it may sound, I was about to fuck her right then and there, but somethin' in me just snapped and brought me back to reality. I heard a baby crying somewhere down the hall and it made me think of Madison. Even though my daughter wasn't an actual baby, she was my baby, and I missed her.

I took a step back and held Ellie out at arm's length. "We can't do this right here, ma'. Let's go in the crib."

She had her eyes closed, and I noted that both of her nipples were poking through her blouse. I couldn't deny she was sexy as hell, and I was having a crazy hard time not snatching her li'l ass up and doing the most, but I had to stay focused.

She ran her tongue across her lips and slowly opened her eyes. "Okay, *Papi*, but be prepared to have your mind blown back. But don't freak out, okay?"

I nodded my head and got a li'l worried. I didn't know what she was up to and the Kings had taken my Mach, so I was completely unprotected. "A'ight, cool. Let's go."

She opened the door and we stepped into a nice li'l cozy apartment that was well furnished and had one too many pictures of the Virgin Mary and Jesus. It also had a lot of crucifixes and candles everywhere, but apart from that, it looked like a nice place to chill.

She took my hand and led me through the house. Nearly every candle we passed, she stopped to light it. She led me further into the back of the house until we came upon a closed brown door. She looked up at me and smiled, then took the knob and turned it. "Surprise!"

I jumped back when the door opened to reveal my cousin Tez sitting on a bed with his shirt off and about four white bandages on his upper body. He took his lighter and lit the big blunt in his mouth before taking a pull from it. Then he looked up at me and smiled. "You know a muthafucka can't kill me." He stood up and walked toward me.

I damn near knocked him over as I wrapped my arms around him and gave him a hug like I hadn't seen him in years. I couldn't believe he was up and walking because the last time I seen him, he was riddled wit' bullets and bleeding profusely. "Nigga, how you get out the hospital so quick?" I asked, taking a step back and looking him over. I'd caused him wounds to start bleeding under his bandages again because I had hugged him so hard.

He pointed the blunt at Ellie. "She told me them people were coming to snatch me up and we needed to get the fuck out of that hospital, so she helped me up out of there after they stitched me up. Then, once we got here, her cousin Mardi finished getting me right. I owe these hoez, man. Fo' real."

That was one thing about Tez: he didn't understand calling a female a bitch or a ho was wrong. He thought it was the most natural thing in the world, and I found myself constantly correcting him on that shit. But this time I didn't have to because Ellie was all over him.

She slammed her hand on her hip and popped her neck back. "Hold on now, *Papi,* because I ain't no ho. Neither is my cousin. You have to show us more respect than that, Tez, okay?"

He put his hand up to his mouth. "Damn. My bad. I ain't mean it like that. I just appreciate y'all, is all."

Ellie rolled her eyes. "Uh-huh. I bet. Anyway, where is Mardi?"

Tez sat back on the bed and took a hit of the blunt while Ellie started to tend to his bloody bandages. "She had to run down to her crib to get me some more of them Oxy. I'm hurting like a muthafucka, and I can't take this pain. I can't wait 'til she get back." He closed his eyes and took a deep breath.

As if on cue, Mardi came through the back door, closing and then locking it. "*Lo siento, Papi.* I didn't mean to take so long, but I'm here now." She opened the pill container and handed Tez two pills.

He took them, set them on the bedside table, and got to crushing them up. "Racine, I swear I see why them rapper niggaz be tooting these muthafuckas. When I hit this shit all the pain leaves my body. I mix this shit wit' that heroin, and it get me right." He continued to crush them up before taking a playing card and tooting up one line after the next. After he finished, he turned back to me with a serene smile on his face. "Damn. I heard about yo' moms. That's fucked up, nigga. You already know we finna body Rayjon ass. Ellie got the hook-up. She finna lace us wit' everything we need." He cheesed and closed his eyes, leaning back on the bed.

Ellie came and grabbed my hand. "Damn, Tez, you talk too much. Now you ruined the surprise I had for him." She rolled her eyes. "Come on, baby." She led me through the house by my hand until we got to another closed door that she opened and pulled me inside of. The bedroom didn't have any furniture inside of it, but it had five trunks. Ellie knelt in front of one and opened it.

"They just got all new stuff at the academy, and all of this is old. They were just going to let it sit up in storage until I gave the property sergeant a nice li'l lap dance and a little head. The last part I'm not so proud of, but after Tez put me up on game about y'all's situation, I wanted to help by any means. Then, once I get y'all right, I want you to help me get the police back that murdered my brother. I want their whole family to pay for killing him, but that'll come later." She held up an all-black bulletproof vest that had POLICE written across the front of it and handed it to me. "Here you go, *Papi*."

I took it out of her hand and noted right away it felt a li'l heavy. I put it right on over my t-shirt and latched it in place. I took a few steps with a smile on my face, then came over by her and knelt down, looking through the trunk and seeing it was filled wit' vests. I got to thinking about E and Wayne right away. It was enough vests in there to protect our whole crew and then some. "What's in them other trunks?" I asked, curious.

She was already opening them up. "This one got all of their old service .9 millimeters. That one has nine AR-15s inside of it. This one is filled with ammo and explosives. Bottom line, you can do some real damage here. I also got uniforms and a bunch of other stuff for you to hit licks with. All I ask is after you are done handling your bitness that you will help me handle mine, because that is extremely important to me." She stepped forward, and pulled me up to her, looking me in the eyes. "Do we have a deal, Racine? Huh?"

A part of me was wondering why she didn't go outside and have that army of goons help her get revenge for her brother, but then I saw her giving all this stuff to them and it taking away from our cartel, so I just kept my questions to myself since it wouldn't be beneficial to ask them. Instead I stepped forward and sucked on her lips, running my hands all over her round ass, squeezing it. With her lips still attached to mine, I looked into her eyes and told her what she needed to hear. "Ellie, I got you. When I'm done handling this bitness, I'ma make every muthafucka pay that had somethin' to do wit' yo' brother being killed. Whatever it will take to make you feel better."

"Even if that means killing the grand jury that acquitted the son of a bitch that killed him?"

I swallowed and had to think about that for a second because it sounded like she already had her mind made up for the long run. I really didn't know what I was getting myself into, but once again I needed everything that was in that room, so I had to do what I had to do. "It don't matter what it is or who it is. I got you," I said, kissing her again.

She blinked her eyes and tears sailed down her cheeks. "Do you promise me that?"

I nodded. "I promise."

Afterward, Mardi pulled a Durango around to the alley and we loaded everything up into her truck before Ellie dropped me and Tez off at my house out in Riverdale. Once we unloaded everything, and before I retired to the house for the night, she made me promise her again, and I did. I really didn't know what I was getting myself into nor who she really was, but my word was everything.

Sometimes telling a person what they want to hear can come back to haunt you. In my case, it was worse than that.

Chapter 5

That night Kenosha woke me up pushing me on the chest with tears in her eyes. "Racine. Racine. Get up, baby. I need you to put me to sleep because I can't go on my own. I feel sick. Please!" she begged, straddling me. Then she leaned down and bit into my neck. It was then I noted she was naked because her hard nipples pressed into my chest and her hot skin molded into mind. Being that it was the middle of the night, I was already hard and ready to go. I think I needed somethin' like that to take my mind off what I was faced with. My mind was clouded, and some good pussy always opened me right up.

I sat up and flipped Kenosha over, so she was lying on her back. She took her hands and ran them over my muscular chest, then down to my abs. "I need you, daddy. I need you to fuck me to sleep. I ain't slept in so many days."

"I got you, boo." I leaned down and sucked on her neck, then bit it. At the same time, I put my hand between her legs and felt all over her plump, wet pussy. Separating her sex lips, I slipped my middle finger into her hole, moving it in and out while she moaned wit' her head tilted backward.

"Mm, daddy. I need you so bad. Please stop playin' wit' me and fuck me as hard as you can. Put me to sleep! Now!" She opened her legs wider and spread her pussy lips with two of her fingers.

I lowered my head all the way down and slurped her sex lips into my mouth, opening them and sticking my tongue into her as far as it would go, tasting her saltiness that drove me crazy. I always loved the taste of my baby mother's pussy. It drove me insane. I licked up and down her crease, then trapped her clit with my lips, nipping at it wit' my teeth very lightly, but enough to make her hump her ass off the bed and into my mouth.

"Huh! Ooh! Shit, daddy! It feel so good. Keep eating me, daddy. Please!" She opened her thighs even wider. It looked like she was trying to hit the splits wit' her juices oozing out of her.

I was fingering her at full speed now and sucking on her clit, flicking back and forth with my tongue. Her juices coated my chin and dripped from it. "Cum for me, Kenosha. Cum all in daddy's mouth. It's okay, baby." I sucked harder on her clit, and now my fingers were really going into her as fast as I could send them in and out.

"Huh! Uh! Daddy! Mm, shit! Please! Huh!" She humped her ass off the bed and forced my face deep into her center, almost smothering me. But I kept on licking and sucking, driving my fingers in and out of her. "I'm cumming, daddy! I'm cumming! Uh, shit!" She wrapped her thick thighs around my head and got to shaking while I drank from her pussy like we were in the desert and her kat was the only source of liquid that would quench my thirst.

My dick was super hard. I had to get inside of her body. I needed some of that pussy. I needed her to heal me wit' her oven as only she could. I was trying to escape from my reality, if only for the moment, so I jumped on top of her and spread her thighs, running my dick head up and down her crease before slowly sinking into her kitty like a hot knife into butter. I bit into my bottom lip wit' my eyes closed because that shit felt so damn good. "Mm, Kenosha. I'm finna beat this shit up. I promise, boo." I pulled all the way back and slammed my pipe home, hitting rock bottom before pulling back and doing it again and again, getting ready to murder that kat like I always did.

Kenosha opened her mouth with her eyes wide open. They continued to roll into the back of her head the harder I hit that shit. "Uh! Uh! Uh! Daddy! Yes! Fuck me harder! Harder, daddy! Please! Uh! Uh! Uh! Yes! Yes! Uh, shit! It. Feels. So. Good!" She wrapped her legs around my waist as I went into my zone, trying to take away the pain of my situation through the use of her box.

I clenched my teeth and got to going as fast and hard as I could, diving deep into her wetness. The headboard knocked into the wall wit' a vengeance. It sounded like somebody was in the room jumping up and down on the bed, as if they were a little kid the way the springs were squeaking like crazy. Her pussy walls sucked at me, milking my pipe, and caused me to bite harder into the bottom of my lip and dig deeper into her pussy, especially after I threw her right leg on my shoulder and went into beast mode. "You want daddy to put you to sleep? Huh?" *Bam. Bam. Bam. Bam. Bam. Bam. Bam. Bam.*

"Uh! Fuck, yes! Ooh, daddy! Uh. Uh. Uh. Uh. Yes. Uh! Shit! Daddy! Daddy! Daddy! Fucking me. Uh! You. Fucking. Me. So. Hard! Uh, shit! I'm. Cumming! Daddy! I'm Cumming. Uh!"

I threw her left leg on my shoulder and got to going so fast and hard my hips were a blur. The sound of our skins slapping together was loud in the room, along with the scent of our sexes. I looked down and saw the way her nipples were standing at attention, brought my head down, and sucked on them while I pounded her out.

The next thing I knew, I felt my abs lock up and my balls got tight. The feeling between her legs got to be better and better. I went faster and faster and as hard as I could, and then I couldn't take it no more.

I pushed her knees to her chest, slammed into her pussy three hard times, and got to cumming back-to-back. "Um! Um! Um! Um! Shit, Kenosha."

After I pulled out, she simply rolled over to her side, grabbed her pillow, and fluffed it. "Thank you, daddy." In less than five minutes she was out like a light and snoring loud enough for me to hear her. I leaned down and kissed her on that big booty before lying on my side of the bed with my eyes pinned on the ceiling, just thinking about Madison.

The next thing I knew, I was out like a light.

***

The next day I met up wit' Rayjon and two of his niggaz at Washington Park in the parking lot a li'l way from the swimming pools. I pulled up in an all-black Tahoe truck I was renting, and he pulled up in an all-red Lexus with black limo tints on it. The sun was beaming, and there were so many people out and on their way to the swimming pools it looked like it was a block party or something.

I jumped out of my truck and got into the back of Rayjon's Lexus with one of his henchmen on each side of me. After I was situated in the middle, they closed the door and Rayjon turned around and pressed a big Mossberg pump into my chest before curling his upper lip. "Nigga, you got my first order of payment, or am I killing yo' ass right here and right now?" he said, pumping the weapon.

I felt my heart beating faster, not from fear of this nigga killing me, but from the hatred I had for his bitch-ass. I wasn't really worried about him bodying me right then. I had one of them police Kevlar vests on that Ellie had gotten from the academy. On top of that, I knew Rayjon was all about his money. I felt like he wasn't gon' try and kill me until I had paid him in full and brought him at least one of the two heads he wanted me to bring him.

I tried to remove the barrel from my chest, but that just made him shove it into me even harder. "Rayjon, chill, nigga. I got the first million in the backseat of my truck right now. It's in a Gucci book bag."

He looked me over closely. "Why the fuck you ain't bring it over here wit' you? What the fuck you on?" he snarled at me.

I mugged this nigga with anger. "What can I be on when you got a pump to my chest and these fuck-niggaz on the side of me, waiting on me to be on bullshit? Just have one of them go and grab it off my backseat."

He looked me over closely, then nodded his head at the dude on my right side. "Go snatch that bag up. You see anything fishy, just wave and I'ma blow this nigga's chest off. Word is bond," Rayjon said, scrunching his face up at me.

There were two families of people who walked past the car, trying to look into it before the dude got out and went to my truck. In the background I could hear the voice of Biggie Smalls spitting out of Rayjon's speakers, which blew my mind because it was late 2018 and I didn't even think niggaz still listened to Big like I did.

"What's good wit' my daughter, nigga?" I asked, feeling him press the barrel harder into my chest. I was missing Madison like crazy and had caught myself shedding tears over her a few times as of late. I needed my baby. Being without her was driving me crazy.

Rayjon sucked his teeth. "Nigga, until you pay me what you owe me, she my daughter. So, my daughter is doing good. She finally woke up and ate some cereal today. She been asking about you and shit, but I don't answer them questions."

As he was finishing up, the nigga he sent to retrieve the money out of the back of my car returned with the book bag and handed it to him.

"I ain't count it, boss, but it is full of one-hunnit dollar bundles."

Rayjon took it and threw it on the passenger's seat. "Oh, I ain't worried about it. If it ain't all there, I'ma knock Madison's brains out her head and put that shit on YouTube." He laughed and then stopped and mugged me. "Averie been in touch wit' you yet?"

Averie was supposed to have been his wife, but she'd shitted on that nigga for me and helped me clean his safe out. I guess he was so salty behind all of shit that he wanted me to kill her and bring him her head. I viewed that nigga as a sucka. What type of nigga wanted to kill a female because she wasn't fuckin' wit' him no more or she chose another nigga? Far as tapping his safe, well, that was just a part of the game. Everybody knew when a nigga was in the game, nobody was to be trusted with all his passwords or safe houses. To me that nigga had fucked his self.

I shook my head. "Nall, she ain't hollered at me in damn near a month now. I think it's gon' come down to me finding her. But I'ma do whatever it takes, believe that."

He shrugged his shoulders. "I don't give a fuck what you do. You already got the deadline I gave you. You let that hit you in the ass, then you popped, and so is yo' shorty." He sucked his teeth and looked out the window for a second as five thick-ass redbones walked past the car in their two-piece bathing suits that had G-string bottoms. I mean, I couldn't even see the strings because their asses were so big. They looked over his

Lexus, but since they couldn't see inside of it, they kept on walking with their asses jiggling. Even at gunpoint I turned around to peep them before shaking my head.

"You remember I told you I wanted you to hit a few licks for me that wouldn't count toward yo' debt to me, right?" Rayjon said, moving the barrel up to my Adam's apple.

I was so heated I felt like trying to snatch that Mossberg out of his hands and blowing him and them other niggaz's heads off. He was treating me like a bitch, and I ain't like it one bit. Had he not had my daughter, I think I would have tried to kill him when I walked over to his Lexus. I was feeling softer than Charmin tissue. Not only did this nigga have my seed, but he was treating me like a straight pussy, and it was killing my soul. I swallowed, and my Adam's apple scraped against the barrel. "Yeah, I remember you saying that. What about it?"

He took the pump away from me and laid it across his lap, then handed me a piece of paper. "You gon' pull a lick tonight at this address. They got a safe behind a washing machine in the basement. It got four kilos of heroin in there and eighty thousand dollars. I know just how much is in there because they work under one of my clients. My client want the whole house murdered. That's every single person wit' no mercy. There should be four people there tonight. You gon' hit them up after one in the morning and before two. I want all the spoils in my lap by two o'clock tomorrow. You dig that?"

I took the address and slid it in my pocket. "Let me talk to my daughter, Rayjon. I ain't seen her in a few days now. This shit killing me, bruh." I looked him straight in the eyes and he held my gaze for a long time before shaking his head.

"Look, you handle this bitness tonight and I'll let you holla at her for a few minutes tomorrow. Now, that's the best I can do, nigga, and never call me bruh again. I ain't yo' brother. I'm gon' be the nigga to put you in that pine box. Ain't no brother of mine get down like you do. My mother would have murdered you in the cradle if she ever detected how disloyal you was gon' turn out to be, bitch-nigga."

Soon as he said the word bitch, he accidentally spit on my face and lip. I wiped that shit off quick. I hated dudes even touching me, so for this nigga to have spit on me, a nigga would have trouble imagining what I wanted to do to him. I curled my upper lip. "A'ight, bet those. I'ma handle this bitness, then you let me holla at my daughter, and we'll go from there."

He picked the Mossberg back up off the seat and aimed it at my left eye. "Nigga, I can't wait to blow yo' shit back. Just to watch yo' brains smoking on the pavement is gon' be a treasure for me." He hawked a loogie and spit it dead in my face. It landed on the right side of my cheek, right next to my nose, and when it dripped down to my lip I damn near lost my mind. "Now get yo' punk ass out of my whip and get my shit!" With that, I was pushed out.

I landed on my back after hitting my elbow and watched his car squeal out of the parking lot with everybody watching him.

Chapter 6

About two hours later that fool Wayne hit me up, and we met up on 104th and Cottage Grove in front of the Gyro Shack. He pulled behind my Tahoe in a blue-and-black Benz truck with E sitting in the passenger's seat already eating on some Checker fries.

I jumped out of my truck and got into the back of theirs, slammin' the door. Wayne turned around with a sly smile on his face.

"Nigga, we thought yo' ass was dead. Muthafuckas ain't heard from you since that shit happened at Gage Park."

E chewed on a handful of fries, then took his pop and sucked it up through the straw before burping and hitting his self on the chest. "Where the fuck you wind up going when we split up?" he asked, then pulled out a knot of hunnit dollar bills.

I shook my head. "I ran into this old man's crib, then called Ellie to come and get me. Oh, and I called all them fire trucks and police and shit to create a diversion, so I could get up out of there. Where y'all go?"

Wayne started laughing. "Them niggaz chased us all the way across Halstead. We wound up running in the fire station over there, and two firemen called the police on they ass. Before the police could get there, we ran and jumped on the El train. That shit was wild, but muthafuckas still alive, so it's good. What's the word wit' Tez? I heard homie out of the hospital? That's what's up."

I nodded, then lowered my head and shook it. "Look, we on bitness tonight. We gotta bust a move for this nigga Rayjon so I can work on getting my daughter back. I'm down another million now, so we gotta hit some licks and make some moves. Y'all said y'all was wit' me, so what's it gon' be? I need to know right now."

E opened his door. "Look, I'm 'bout to run in here and get a few gyros, then I'm down for whatever. If we gotta kill, stick a nigga, it don't matter because I'ma be full. I'll follow yo' lead, Racine. That's my word, nigga."

Wayne sucked his teeth as E got out of the truck and disappeared into the restaurant. "I got a lick for us, too. We can get about a hunnit and fifty gees and at least a couple kilos of dog food. We might have to hit some niggaz up, though." He rubbed his chin and looked like he was in deep thought.

I shrugged my shoulders. "I don't even give a fuck. My daughter's life at stake. I'll hit anybody long as it ain't none of my niggaz." I meant that, too. I was to the point where everybody was in jeopardy.

Wayne nodded his head. "Look, you just got at some niggaz in honor of my daughter wit' me, so I'll most definitely return that favor and then some. I got a lot of love and respect for you, Racine. You and that nigga E and Tez. I'm riding wit' you niggaz with every ounce of blood in my veins until my last breath, that's my word. So just tell me what you wanna do and I got yo' back."

After he said those words to me, E got back in the car wit' a bag of gyros. Even though I was sick at the moment missing and thinking about Madison, as soon as I smelled the food, I got super hungry. He offered me one, and I damn near started eating it before taking the paper from around it.

Twelve in the morning seemed like it came real fast that night. I'd reached out to Tez and asked him if he wanted to ride out wit' us to handle this bitness, but it turned out he wasn't strong enough just yet. Plus, he was so doped up on painkillers I couldn't count on him to have our backs like he usually did, so I decided to pull this lick with just me, Wayne, and E. Besides, my li'l niggaz was head-bustahs, anyway. Adding Tez to the mix would have just been overkill.

It started raining just after midnight, and I was cool wit' that because it seemed like when it rained outside people became more sleepy and lazy. They also tended to leave windows open, so they could hear the rain better, and this was how we wound up getting into the house Rayjon wanted us to hit that night.

We got there at about one fifteen, and by that time it was raining so hard I could barely see in front of me. The lightning lit up the sky for a brief second before the thunder roared behind it. We were rolling in a brown Ford Aerostar van. E parked three houses down from the one we were about to hit, in the alley next to a green garage that had a dead dog laying in front of it. I slid open the side door of the van with my white ski mask slid down my face already. I reached on the side of me and grabbed the automatic shotgun that held five slugs at a time. In my inside fatigue pocket was about thirty more red-shelled bullets. If I had to use every one of them, I would wit' no hesitation. I already was double-breasted wit' two Glock .40s, one in each shoulder holster, and the bulletproof vest strapped in place. Put simply, I was ready for action, and so was my two li'l homies.

I jumped out and stepped over the dog, but Wayne must not have seen it because he stepped right on its body and jumped in the air like he was about to freak out. "What the fuck is that?" He hollered, taking baby steps toward the dead animal.

E came around the van and looked down on the dog with his mask already on. "Nigga, that a dead pit bull. Come on, let's handle this bitness and get the fuck out of here. The niggaz over here hate black people. I don't know what that fool Rayjon getting us into." He started jogging down the wet alley with me and Wayne close behind him. He had a Tech .9 in his gloved hand, and Wayne had another Uzi with an extended clip. I guess we could say we was looking to do some damage.

The backyard had a big metal fence we had to jump. On a normal day it wouldn't have been hard to do, but since it was raining so bad it made everything slippery. On top of that, the wind was blowing like crazy, whistling and the whole nine yards. When I went to get my grip on the gate at first, I slipped off, but then instead of trying to climb I took a step back, jumped, and scaled the top of it. Wayne leaped over it wit' no problem, but E took his time. I think the homie was afraid of busting his shit, and I couldn't blame him.

After it was all said and done we wound up over the fence and in the backyard of our mark's crib, jogging through the wet grass until we stood wit' our backs against the red-bricked house. Wayne crouched down in front of me, looking up at it. "Bruh, y'all chill here. I'm finna see if I can find an open window or somethin'. If I do, I'ma come back and let y'all know."

He took off along the side of the house while I looked up at it. It appeared everybody inside was asleep because from my vantage point I couldn't see any lights on inside. I smiled at that under my mask because to me the easiest lick to hit was the one where everybody was sleeping. If Rayjon was saying he wanted everybody in the house dead, then we shouldn't have any risk at all completing that task.

Wayne came back about two minutes later and crouched down on the side of me. "A'ight, look. They got a window that's open in the pantry. I'm finna slide through that muthafucka and come right up and open the door. It's closer to the back of the house, so y'all should hear if anything go wrong. If so, kick this do' in and come through that bitch busting. A'ight?"

I nodded, and he disappeared. I looked over as E cocked his Tech and got closer to me.

"I'm wit' you, big homie. We gon' get yo' daughter back, nigga. Just you watch." He tapped my shotgun wit' his Tech and lowered his eyes into slits.

Just then I heard the lock turn on the back door, and when it opened the scene before me blew my mind. Wayne had a naked nigga by his throat wit' his Uzi inside of the dude's mouth. He brought him all the way outside and flung him to the ground in the rain, then straddled him.

The dude threw his hands into the air. "Hey, man, please don't do this to me. I'm. Uh!"

Wayne started to beat him over the head with the handle of his Uzi. The first blow cracked his forehead down the middle and blood skeeted out of the wound, but that didn't stop him from pounding his head in more and more like a psycho while the man kicked his legs and tried to get up. Wayne was having none of that. He held him by the throat and continued to bash his head in with anger until the man was unmoving and lay in a pile of blood.

I didn't know what the fuck was going on. I was too busy worrying somebody else was going to come out of the house and see us and call the police before we could handle our bitness. "What the fuck, bruh?" I said, looking down at the dead Mexican dude who lay in the grass with his eyes wide open.

Wayne stood up with blood all over his clothes. "Caught his bitch-ass on his way upstairs as I was coming downstairs to open the door for y'all." He sucked his teeth. "They having some type of orgy in that bitch. It's so much moaning going on, and it don't smell like nothin' but dick and pussy. I don't know how many people in there, but it's way more than what Rayjon said it was gon' be. You sure he told you to hit them up at this time?" Wayne asked on his way back into the house.

I nodded. "Hell yeah. He said after one and before two. It's 1:20 right now," I said looking at my phone.

Lightning struck somewhere off in the distance. *Boom!* Then the rain started to come down twice as hard while the wind picked up even more, nearly knocking me over.

E walked over to us looking like he was finna fall. "Man, fuck it, bruh. Let's just go and wet they ass and get this loot. We ain't got all day."

I agreed wit' him. We would have to find out what was what when we got in there.

Wayne nodded and waved us inside. I followed close behind him wit' my shotgun ready for action. I was a little worried about the noise the shots would make, but at the same time the thunder was doing its thing in the sky to mask a little bit of what we were about to put down.

Wayne ran up the stairs and onto the downstairs landing. We wound up in a short hallway that led us through a kitchen and directly into a living room that smelled like heavy sex and was lit up by candles. There had to be at least ten people in there, and they were all fucking like crazy while they banged reggaeton music. I mean they were having good sex, too, because them females were moaning loud. "Aw! Aw! Oh! Yes, *Papi*! Aw! Aw! Mm! *Papi*! *Papi*!"

E flicked on the lights, and as soon as he did the naked tangle of bodies on the floor looked up at us in fear before they began to scramble and scream.

The first Mexican dude jumped up and ran toward .38 Special less than four feet away from him, and I ain't waste no time letting his ass have it. *Boom*! The shotgun lurched backward into me while my bullet spit out of the barrel and slammed into his back, knocking him forward into the wall. Blood splattered across the china cabinet before he fell to his knees and crumbled into a ball, lifeless.

Wayne nodded his head. "Hell yeah! Aye! Everybody get on they muthafuckin' stomachs or everybody die. Now!"

One by one the naked crowd of people turned onto their stomachs. A few of the women whimpered in fear. I was hoping I didn't have to kill none of them. I would body the dudes all day long, but I just felt some type of way about killing a defenseless female. Luckily my li'l homies didn't give a fuck because Rayjon said he wanted the whole house smoked.

I was reeling and knew we had to hurry up and get out of there. I was feeling some type of way because although Rayjon had given me the address, he hadn't given me the name of the main person I was supposed to get all the merch from. So, as far as I knew, it could have been anybody in the house. I leaned down and snatched up a

Mexican dude wit' long hair, putting the barrel under his chin. "Where the fuck is the money and dope at? And don't play wit' me!" I spat.

He shook his head. "Don't have no money or dope. Just got here from Mexico. Please don't kill us," he said, and I saw his knees were shaking.

I pushed him against the wall wit' all of my might and cocked my shotgun, putting the barrel to his throat. "Listen to me, bitch-ass nigga. I ain't got time for these games. Now take me to the money and dope or I'ma kill you. You got one last chance."

He started to piss on himself. The urine came out of his penis and sprayed his inner thigh before coursing down his leg. "Okay, my wallet is on the dresser. You can have all the money. Just please don't kill us."

Wallet? I thought this nigga was out of his mind. How could eighty gees fit in a wallet? I thought maybe he was mixing up his words since he didn't speak English that good. "How much money in yo' wallet, *vato*?"

"My rent money. Six hundred, that's all I have." His knees got weak, causing him to slump to the floor some. I could see he was shaking like he was freezing cold.

E snatched up a naked female, put his Tech to her temple, and pulled the trigger. *Tat-tat-tat!* Her brains flew out of the side of her face and splashed on to the woman lying directly below her. She jumped up and started to scream.

"Ah! *Dios mio!* Ah! *Dios mio!*" She put two hands to her face and looked down at the dead woman in shock.

Wayne stepped forward and knocked her out with a closed fist. *Wham!* Right in her forehead. She slumped to the floor immediately with her eyes rolling into the back of her head. "We ain't playin' wit' you muthafuckas! Now, where is the money and dope at? Y'all got ten seconds to tell us somethin' or everybody in this bitch dying!"

All that came from the crowd of people lying on their stomachs was a bunch of whimpering and crying. I couldn't believe nobody spoke up to save their own lives. It was blowing my wig back.

I snatched up another older dude who had a mean scowl on his face. He looked like he was ready to snap out and pass out at the same time. Grabbing him by the neck just like I did the other dude, I put my lips to his ear. "Where is the money and dope? This my last time asking anybody," I said through clenched teeth.

He shook his head from side to side. "I don't know what you're talking about. There is no dope here. Maybe you want my son. He is a King Pin, not me. He no live here. Just me." His breath smelled like heavy alcohol and pussy mixed together.

I shook my head real hard to try to figure out what I should do. I couldn't believe these muthafuckas wasn't give up the goods after they had seen us kill two people already. Somethin' wasn't right.

"I'm finna tear this bitch up, bruh. It gotta be somethin' here," E said, disappearing into a room down the hallway.

Wayne's eyes lowered into slits. "So, what's the word, bruh? Cuz I'm ready to get to killing these muthafuckas and getting it over wit'." He stood over about four people with his gun aimed down at them, then my phone rang.

I reached into my pocket and picked up the call after seeing it was from an anonymous number. That's what usually came across the screen whenever Rayjon hit me up, and as soon as I put the phone to my ear there was his voice. "Aw, that's my fault, li'l dawg. I got you at the wrong house." He started laughing like somethin' was really funny.

I scrunched my face. "What you mean you got me at the wrong house, nigga?" I was heated. At saying the last part, Wayne perked up and walked toward me with his eyes still on our victims.

He laughed again. "You heard me. Instead of sending you to the lick's house, I sent you to where his people lay they head. Oh well, I guess you'll have to hit both spots tonight. I want every muthafucka in there bodied. Then I want you to get to this right address I'm sending you. You gotta make it there in less than twenty minutes, so hurry up. Yo' daughter's life on the line because you fuckin' wit' my money!" A new address came across my phone and then the line disconnected.

I was mad as a muthafucka. This nigga was sending me off, and because he had my daughter I didn't have no choice other than to do everything

75

he was ordering me to do. Second to that, I didn't like how he was talking on that phone. That was real reckless.

"What we finna do, bruh? Come on and say somethin' because we can't be in this bitch all day. We done already let off too many shots."

E came from down the hallway and threw a bunch of syringes and ropes onto the floor. "Man, this shit look fishy. It seemed like they a bunch of dope fien's, bruh. I ain't finding shit but drug paraphernalia. That's it."

I swallowed and tilted my head back, closing my eyes. "Fuck this bitch-ass nigga!" As much as I didn't want to, I knew I had to do whatever Rayjon was ordering me to do. I didn't know how I was gon' sleep that night, but in that moment, I just had to do what I had to.

"Kill everybody and let's get up out of here. We gotta hit up the right place this nigga just texted me. But he saying he want everybody here dead, so let's go."

I took a step back and upped my shotgun, pressed it to the dude whose neck I was holding a moment ago, and pulled the trigger, feeling the gun jump in my hands. *Boom!* A big hole formed in his stomach before he dropped to the floor, bleeding out. I pumped the shotgun and aimed it downward toward another dude who jumped up and tried to jump through the window. *Boom!* The bullet knocked him forward and caused him to crash through it. All around me E and Wayne where letting their shots ring out on the innocent victims. The smell of gunpowder and blood wafted into the air, making my stomach turn. I didn't mind killing when I had to, but I never liked killing somebody for no reason. I felt like this whole house we murdered this day was for nothin' apart from the games Rayjon wanted to play.

I continued to let my shotgun blast, but made sure I didn't hit no females, only the dudes. Wayne and E handled the dirty work, and after they were done I ran around checking people's pulses to make sure they were gone. After confirming that, we hit it out the back door and hopped the fence. When we got back to the van this time there were about six big-ass rats eating at the dog's carcass. As we ran to get inside the van, I was expecting them to scatter like roaches, but instead they hissed at us with mouths full of blood.

T.J. EDWARDS

Chapter 7

Whom! As soon as I ran into the house I saw there were four dudes sitting around a table with big bottles of tequila in the center of it. I ran at them full-speed with the shotgun's stock pressed against my shoulder. "Everybody get the fuck down now or I'm killing you bitchez! This ain't a game!"

Wayne came from the side of me with his Uzi pointed at them. "Y'all niggaz heard my dude! Get the fuck down! Now!"

In the background the sounds of reggaeton played through the speakers. The men fell to the floor on their stomachs. E ran around pullin' them by their legs until they were in the center of the floor beside each other. The apartment was small and smelled like some strong-ass rock cocaine. It made my stomach hurt right away because I hated the smell of that shit.

I walked over and put the barrel of my shotgun to the back of a heavyset Mexican dude's head. "I wanna know where the money and the dope is, and I wanna know right now. I swear if you play any games wit' me, I'm blowing yo' head clean off your shoulders." I didn't want to prolong this situation. I wanted to be in and out. We had already killed ten people that night. Now there were another four to add to the body count.

The fat dude held his arms straight above his head. "I'll take you to the safe, homes. It ain't that serious. Just don't kill none of my *familia*." He said the last part in Spanish, but I knew he meant family.

I snatched him up. "Let's go then!" Rayjon already told me the safe was in the basement, and even though I didn't trust him at all, I was prepared to pop this fat nigga if he took me anywhere besides the basement, but he didn't.

He took me down the stairs into the dark basement. At seeing it was dark, I wrapped my arm around his neck and held the shotgun under his chin. "Fuck is the light at, nigga?" I asked, tightening my grip on him.

"Ack! Ack! Shit. Calm down, homes. It's hanging on a string right here." As we got to the middle of the basement, he reached up and pulled on the string, illuminating the basement. "The safe is behind the washing machine over there by that sink. All I gotta do is pull it out and go behind it. You can have everything that's in there. It should be a good lick for you and your crew. Just don't hurt nobody."

I pushed him forward real roughly toward the washing machine, causing him to stumble and nearly fall before he caught himself. "Open that bitch up and hurry up!" I reached into my boxer briefs and pulled out a black plastic garbage bag and threw it at him. "Put everything in there and hurry the fuck up. You got two minutes."

He picked up the bag and looked up at me with an evil look on his face, then jogged over to the washing machine and pulled it away from the brick wall, exposing a safe. I kept my eyes on him as he entered the combination, but at the same time it sounded like there was commotion going on upstairs. I couldn't really tell what it was, but something wasn't right.

The fat dude started to load up bundle after bundle of cash into the bag. "Hurry up!" I yelled.

"I am. I am." He filled the bag up faster and faster.

Then I heard a loud bang, followed by a bunch of footsteps. I turned around for a second to look in the direction of the stairs, and boy, why did I do that? I should have never let my guard down. I knew better than that.

Boom! Boom! Boom! Boom! Two bullets slammed into my chest and knocked me on my ass so hard I hit my head on the concrete floor. The shock of the bullets caught me off guard, and my heart was beating faster than I ever remembered it.

Boom! A bullet slammed into the floor right next to my head. *Boom!* This one popped me in the stomach and turned me on my side after knocking the wind out of me.

The fat nigga knelt down to reload his revolver. I couldn't breathe, and time was moving so slow. I knew I had to fight to survive this moment. No matter what, I could not let this nigga kill me this night.

I slowly raised my shotgun, aimed it at him, and pulled the trigger. *Boom!* The fire spit from my barrel, and the bullet flew across the room and landed right in his neck, knocking his head halfway off his shoulders. He did a one-eighty before landing in a pool of blood.

My chest felt hot, and so did my stomach, but thanks to the vest I was able to avoid the actual rounds going into my body. It still hurt like a muthafucka, though. Don't think just because I was wearing a vest it didn't feel like I had been shot, because it did. I felt every slug he popped at me that connected.

Gunshots went off upstairs. I willed myself to get up and grab the bag of money. Kneeling, I saw he'd neglected to put the kilos of dope into the bag, so I did. I cleared the entire safe and made my way upstairs, nearly crashing into E on my way.

"Bruh, what's good? I heard shots," he said with his eyes bucked.

It felt like I had broken a few ribs or something because wit' every step I took it was hard for me to breathe. On top of that my whole torso felt incredibly hot, like it was on fire. I didn't know until later that I had to pick the bullets out of the vest and the indentation they'd made had caused the metal to pierce my skin. "I'm good, bruh. Dude bitch-ass just caught me slipping. What's good up here?" I asked, stepping into the living room.

Wayne was standing over three dead bodies. "I hope you got everything, because these niggaz is dead. We heard shots, thought it was a set-up."

I looked down at the men and saw Wayne had shot them all in the face and head area. Blood was all over the floor, along wit' brain and meat. I shook my head. "Let's get up out of here, bruh. I got everythang."

The ride back was the longest ride ever for me. I was so far into my head I couldn't think straight. I felt sick. That was fourteen people dead in one night. I knew Chicago was about to be on fire, not to mention I didn't know who it was we'd just hit up. As far as I knew I could have been creating more enemies and more drama for myself and my crew.

I felt like I was trapped and there was no way out. I wanted my daughter back so bad. I missed her. I just wanted to hold her in my arms, to feel her wrap her little ones around my neck and nuzzle her face into the crux of my neck like she always did.

***

I met up wit' Rayjon at the lakefront the next day right before two in the afternoon. He pulled up alongside my Tahoe in an all-black Hummer with what seemed like six armed dudes inside of it. As soon as they parked he got out of his Hummer and came over to the driver's side of my truck, wiggling the door handle.

"Open this muthafucka up," he ordered.

I had the bag of merch sitting on my passenger's seat and my .40 caliber gun on my lap. Before I opened the door, I looked around at all of the people carrying on wit' their day at the lakefront as if they didn't have a care in the world. The sun was shining, and it had to be about ninety degrees outside, which was hot as hell for April in Chicago. I didn't think Rayjon had enough guts to body me in front of all those spectators, but then again, I didn't really know because at times he acted like he was off his rocker.

I opened the door and he pulled me out of the truck and shoved me toward the Hummer. Two of his men snatched me up and forced me into the back of it while I watched Rayjon get into my truck and drive off. Seconds later his Hummer was being driven by one of his goons.

We rolled through the city of Chicago for about ten minutes. All the while the only thing I could think about was Madison. I wondered if she was okay. I wondered if she was eating the way she needed to and if Rayjon had laid a finger on my baby. I just missed her so, so much. I hated that I'd slipped up and gotten her and Kenosha involved in the street life I was caught up in. I always tried to keep my dirt away from home. I knew it was a cardinal sin to bring the slums home wit' you.

I started to panic a li'l bit when I saw Rayjon pull into the old bus station repair shop off Marshfield. It had been abandoned for two years and now just looked like an old warehouse with broken glass and over-filled dumpsters in front of it. They had found more than one dead body inside of those dumpsters.

When we got there, there was another car already parked, Rayjon pulled up alongside it in my truck before getting out of it with the black garbage bag in his hand. He snapped his fingers at the Hummer that held me, and the next thing I knew I was being shoved out of the Hummer by one of his big, beefy goons. The sun shined in my face.

Rayjon walked up to me with a mug across his grill. "I see you handled that bitness like you was supposed to, kid. I take it all my money and dope is in this bag?" He held up the bag wit' one hand and smiled.

I nodded. "Where is Madison, man? You said if I handled that bitness you was gon' let me see my daughter," I said, feeling my temper get hot.

He tossed the black bag to one of his beefy goons and smiled at me again. "You know what? I'm a man of my word. I said I was gon' let you see yo' daughter, and I am." He looked toward the red car that had tinted windows. He snapped his fingers and the back door to the car opened. A big, bald nigga got out holding Madison in his arms. He put her to the ground on her feet and let her go.

"Daddy!" She took off running to me. "Daddy!"

She had to be about a hundred feet away. I felt my heart pound in my chest the closer she got to me. I just wanted to hold her so bad. I needed to. I was going crazy without my baby girl. No father should've had to feel like I was feeling. The closer she got to me, the dizzier I got.

"Daddy!"

I squatted down and opened my arms wide. She ran inside of them, crashing into me. As soon as I felt the impact tears fell out of my eyes and sailed down my cheeks. I hugged her tight and held on for a long time while she cried into my neck. "I missed you so much, princess. I been thinking about you every single day since you been gone. Do you understand me?" I loosened my arms a li'l bit, so I could look down into her face. She was fully crying, and it made my heart so heavy.

"I wanna go home wit' you, Daddy. I don't wanna go back wit' those big, scary men. I miss Momma and Grandma. Why do I have to stay wit' them?" She cried harder.

I swallowed and felt like shit. Here my baby girl was being dragged through the mud and there was very little I could do to help her. I felt worse than a pussy. I felt worthless. I felt like somebody should have put a bullet in my head and sent me on my way. I didn't think there was any worse feelin' than the one of not being able to protect my child, especially since she was a girl. I was nuts over Madison. She was my heart and soul.

I pulled her back into my embrace. "You only gotta be wit' them for a li'l while longer, then you can come home wit' Daddy. I promise it won't be that long, baby girl. I'm doing everything I can to make things move faster. I miss you so, so much, and so does Mommy." I kissed her cheek and hugged her while I mugged Rayjon wit' hatred. I was gon' get that nigga. If it was the last thing I did, I was gon' get him back for hurting my baby girl. Killing my mother was one thing. I was gon' murder him in cold blood for that alone. But hurting my daughter was on a whole other level.

"Why isn't Mommy here? Did she not wanna see me? She don't want me home because I told her I love you the most before?" she whimpered with her chest heaving up and down. The tears continued to fall as she looked me in the face.

I felt like I wanted to scream and break down myself. I needed to heal my daughter. I needed to prove to her we still loved her, and we wanted her home, that this circumstance had nothin' to do wit' her. I could tell emotionally it was so hard for her to understand everything. I mean, she was only seven years old. I held her in front of me and moved her curly hair out of her face. It had once been in a neat ponytail, but somehow it had fallen all the way out of its ponytail holder and covered her face. I rubbed her cheeks with my thumbs, wiping her tears away.

"Baby, Mommy misses you just as much as I do. We both cry for you every night, and we can't wait for you to come back home, but it's up to me to get you there because I was bad, and I gotta pay these people back before you can come back to me. This is all my fault, not Mommy's, okay?"

She nodded her head. "Okay. But won't you hurry up, so I can get back home to you? You love me, don't you?" At saying this, she put her little hands up to my face and held it, looking me in the eyes wit' her head turned slightly to the side.

I felt like I melted. My daughter always had that effect on me. "Yes, I love you, baby girl, and Daddy gon' get you home very, very soon. I promise." I mugged Rayjon, who was now smoking on a fat blunt and eyeing me wit' a smile spread across his face. Somehow, some way I was gon' make that nigga pay for all of this. I could never accept all this lying down like a pussy-type nigga. Never.

Madison nodded her head and lay her head on my chest, hugging me tight. "I love you so much, Daddy. You're still my favorite."

Hearing that made me even more weak, yet mad at the same time.

Rayjon held his hand in the air and snapped his fingers, and the big, beefy goon walked over and snatched my daughter up into his arms. "Ah! Daddy!" Madison screamed and began kicking her legs and swinging her arms wildly.

I hopped to my feet, cocked back, and punched that big nigga straight in his jaw with so much force. *Crack*! As soon as I made contact with his jaw, he dropped my daughter and I caught her. He fell backward and landed with a thud in the dirt, causing dust to fly into the air. Knocked out cold.

I held Madison in my arms, looking down on him. "Don't you ever yank her out my arms like that, nigga! This my baby right here!" I growled and got ready to kick him in the chest.

Rayjon came out of his holsters with two .44 Desert Eagles. Behind him, his men also upped their numerous weapons. He walked over to me with his gun pointed at my forehead. "Damn, Racine. You got all this heart that I can definitely use for my cartel, but you just had to cross me wit' that bitch." He shook his head. "You could have been a rich nigga fuckin' wit' me, but you ain't got no patience, and in this game you gotta exercise patience." He snapped his fingers. "Give me that li'l girl or I'm blowing her head off right here and right now and still leaving you alive. I'll have my niggaz go snatch Kenosha up and we'll repeat the same process, but one way or another you gon' get me my three million and them two headz. Now, give her to me! Now, Fuck-nigga!"

I lowered her to the ground. She kept her arms wrapped around my neck, holding onto me for dear life. The feeling crushed my soul. I knew right then and there I would do anything to never feel what I was feeling. My baby needed me, and there was nothin' I could do for her other than release her back into the hands of her captors. I felt lower than sewage the rats had pissed in.

"No, Daddy, I don't wanna go back wit' them. Please don't make me. I'm begging you!" she sobbed before shaking as of she were freezing cold.

Before I could respond to that, Rayjon yanked her up by the back of her shirt and pushed her to one of his men. The muscle-bound man picked her up and proceeded to walk her back to the red car wit' tinted windows just as the other dude I'd knocked out stirred in the dirt and sat up, shaking the cobwebs out of his head.

Rayjon walked over to him and aimed his .44 right into his face. *Boom! Boom! Boom!* "Soft-ass nigga!" The bullets slammed into the goon's face blew apart before knocking him backward. He lay in a pool of blood with his left leg kicking for a few seconds. Then it stopped.

Rayjon walked over to me with a mug on his face. "I'm gon' send you a text tomorrow night for a lick I want you to hit. Handle this bitness while at the same time getting my next million together for me. This shit ain't a game, Racine. You want yo' daughter back, then you won't piss me off more than you already have." He stepped into my face and pressed his forehead to mine, clenching his jaw. "I hate you Chicago niggaz. It's gon' feel so sweet bodying yo' punk-ass."

I stepped forward and pressed my forehead harder into his. "Nigga, if you ain't have my daughter, I swear this picture would look real different. Just like you hate us Chicago niggaz, we hate you niggaz from out east." I clenched my jaw, feeling like I was finna crush my teeth because I was doing it so hard. I wanted to kill Rayjon worse than I ever wanted to kill any man in my whole entire life. I could literally taste his kill. I hated this nigga so much I felt like I could eat this nigga, on some cannibalism shit.

He grunted and bumped me out of the way, walking off toward the car that had my daughter inside of it. "Wait for my text and get my money, Racine. Time is ticking." He put his hand in the air and turned his finger in a circle. "Let's go!"

They loaded up into their whips and smashed away. I watched the red car for a long time until well after it disappeared wit' Madison inside of it, then I got behind the wheel of my Tahoe and let a few tears fall down my cheeks.

I had to get my baby back. I just had to.

Chapter 8

After leaving the scene wit' my daughter, I felt like I needed to check in on Jill to make sure she was doing okay. The last time I'd seen her she was being gunned down in front of me. Kenosha made it her bitness to check in on her every day, and the report she had given me two days ago was Jill was still on life support. I needed to see her. I missed her, and even though we had never been more than just friends, I cared about her a lot to the point there were feelings there for her. I just didn't understand what kind they were yet. I was on my way to the hospital to see her when I pulled up to a red light just after it flashed yellow. I took the time to send Kenosha a quick text to let her know I would be home tonight after I checked in on Jill.

It was like she was sitting by the phone waiting on me to text because she responded immediately.

Baby, I'm sorry to tell you, but Jill died this morning. They need a family member to go and identify her body. Please don't be mad at me for not tellin you sooner.

I bucked my eyes while looking over the screen, then simply shook my head and felt like I had lost a good friend. First her children were gunned down, and then her. Life was a bitch. I didn't know how to feel or what to do.

I was literally stuck there in my zone when the car behind me started to blow its horn. I looked up, saw the light was green, and stepped on the gas, pulling off. I was imagining Jill's face and all the things we did together. She had a good heart and fell for me quick. In my opinion she was just a single mother who was out in the cold world of Chicago trying to make it with the odds stacked against her. When I figured things out wit' Madison, I would have to find out who it was that had targeted her and her children, murdering them.

I was just pulling up to my house when a call came through on the phone that gave me chills. It was from Averie, Rayjon's so-called wife and the female whose head he was calling for. I felt like my heart was about to jump out of my mouth. I answered it immediately.

Kenosha must've been looking out of the window, saw my truck, and decided to come to me.

"Hello, Averie? What's good, girl?"

"Baby, I miss you so much. It's been crazy without you. I miss that pipe. Do you miss me?" she asked just as Kenosha came to the truck and knocked on the window.

I waved Kenosha off and covered the phone wit' my hand. "Kenosha, go in the house. I'll be in there in a minute. This is bitness." I held up the phone, so she could see what I meant.

She poked her lip out. "Aw. Baby, I just wanna make sure you're okay. We've been through a lot and we need each other. You ain't going nowhere else tonight, is you?"

I shook my head. "Nall. I'll be in the house in a minute. Now go, baby, damn."

She bucked her eyes, then slapped the glass of the front passenger's window. "Fine then, Racine! I'll see you in the house." She waved me off and jogged back up the stairs. I watched her ass jiggle in her thin nightgown. My baby mother was strapped, and I knew I had to hit that shit this night.

I put my ear back to the phone. "Hello, Averie? You still there?"

"Mm. Yeah, baby boy, I'm still here. Now, do you miss me or what? Or are you still playin' games wit' that li'l girl you call yo' baby mother? I thought you liked this vet pussy?" she laughed.

I took a deep breath and exhaled slowly. Averie was hip to the game, and I didn't want to scare her off under no circumstances. I needed her to meet up wit' me, and I didn't know where I was gon' take it from there, but I knew that was first things first. "Hell yeah, I missed you, baby. And you already know ain't nothin' like that vet pussy, especially the kind that's between yo' legs. You know you my mommy," I said, playing into her li'l fetish. Averie had this thing where she liked to think of me as her little boy while I beat that pussy up. She was obsessed wit' our age difference. She had to be about fifteen years older than me, and I loved that because, honestly, older women knew how to get down in that sack.

"Mm. Baby, don't be talking to me like that. You already know that kind of talk drives me crazy. Let's meet up tonight."

My heart started beating even faster. If she was trying to meet up, that mean she was in town.

If she was in town, that meant if I had to, I could give Rayjon what he wanted from her, which was her head. I didn't know for a fact I could go through wit' cutting her head off her body, but I'd have to play that by ear because at the end of the day, I would do anything for my daughter wit' no hesitation. I had love for Averie, but I didn't love nobody more than Madison. That included Kenosha and myself.

"Man, we can meet up wherever you want to, Averie. I miss you so much. I just need to see you." I prayed she took the bait.

"Okay then. Well, I'm close to you. I'm not actually in Chicago, but I'm sending you over a text right now. Meet me at this address in an hour. Oh, and bring some energy, because I need your body like never before."

The address came through on the phone, and I almost fainted. I noted she was in Waukegan, which was about thirty minutes from where I was in Chicago.

I ran into the house and straight to my bedroom. Kenosha had been in the kitchen putting my food into the microwave. "Look, baby, I gotta go handle this bitness in honor of our child. If I can bust this move the right way, we'll be real close to getting her back." I loaded up three pistols and a serrated knife on me and was on my way back out of the crib, texting E and Wayne on my way to my Tahoe truck wit' Kenosha on my heels.

"Baby, you said you was finna stay in tonight. Damn, I never see you. You ain't the only one going through this shit. I miss her just as much as you do, and I need somebody. I'm pregnant, Racine! Did you forget that?" she hollered as I started the engine on my truck.

"Fuck!" I said, slamming both of my hands on the steering wheel as she made her way back into the house. I jumped out of the truck and ran behind her, catching her arm before she closed the door. "Look, Kenosha. I'm sorry, baby, I just gotta follow this lead. I know you in this house struggling and you tired of being there alone, but don't think I'm in these streets just playing around and not handling bitness, because I am." I lowered my head. "I saw our daughter today, baby. Rayjon let me hold her for a few minutes, and it was the best thing in the world. She's doing okay. I told her you love and miss her, and we will be getting her back real soon."

Kenosha bucked her eyes. "You saw her today? And you didn't Facetime wit' me? What's yo' problem, Racine? Don't you know not seeing her is killing me? I'm her mother, and I feel so helpless." She blinked back tears and shook her head. "You know what? It's all too much. I can't take this shit! I can't do this everyday without you, without knowing what's going on with her every step of the way!" She ran into the house and slammed the door, locking it. "Go do whatever you gotta do but get my baby back! I'm tired of this shit!"

I couldn't help but shed tears the whole way to Waukegan. I felt like I was fucking up, and I didn't know how to improve. Emotionally Kenosha was being abandoned. I knew that for a fact. She needed me there every second of every day while we were going through this, and I had not been there for her the way I was supposed to be. I was asking for her to endure a lot with not enough light at the end of the tunnel. I didn't know how I was supposed to be in the house consolin' her while at the same time getting our daughter back. I knew she was pregnant, and that made her even more needy of me, but I didn't know how to make it all work out, so everybody felt fulfilled and uplifted while we were all going through our own individual challenges, with the root of it all being Rayjon attacking our family in the coldest way possible. One way or the other, he found a way to deeply wound us to our family's core.

I pulled up in front of the duplex Averie had given me the address to. I turned the truck off and looked over the block that appeared to be deserted. It was about eight at night and the sun was just starting to go down. I texted her that I was outside and made sure I had all my weapons on me. I didn't know what I was going to do in that moment. I planned on playing it all by ear and just taking things as they came.

Averie appeared on the porch about a minute later with a red silk robe on. It was so short it showed off her thick caramel thighs. I ain't gon' even lie and say her body didn't appeal to me, because it did. I knew how she got down in that bedroom, and just thinking about her sex game was making me feel some type of way, and that was crazy because I knew the mission that stood before me. It was crazy how my dick really did have a mind of its own.

She waved me to her. "Come on, baby, before I get bit by a damn mosquito." She rubbed her arms and walked back into the house, that big-ass booty shaking a li'l bit wit' each step she took. I shook my head. Damn, it wasn't nothin' like a thick-ass woman. I just appreciated her kind.

I got out of my truck and followed her inside after taking one last look over my shoulder at the quiet neighborhood. She was standing right in the entrance of the doorway, and when I got partway in she took my hand and pulled me all the way inside, closing the door behind me.

Almost immediately I was bum-rushed by three females with pistols in their hands. Before I could make a move, they got the jump on me, and I had two guns pressed up against my throat and one at my chest. I felt like I had been set up. I was sick.

"What's this all about, Averie?" I asked, looking over the chocolate sista's head and back to Averie.

Averie shook her head and held up a hand. "Be cool, Racine. I just gotta be careful because I know that nigga Rayjon floating around Chicago. I also know he done made some kind of contact wit' you. I just don't know how much." She walked up to me and started to search me. "I just gotta make sure I'm straight and you ain't finna blindside me. Not saying I don't trust you or nothin', but I just know how that nigga get down.

I grew up wit' him and his family, and them Edwards is crazy."

I swallowed and started to panic. I knew when she discovered all the weapons on me the shit would hit the fan. "That nigga been at my head ever since he been back in town. That's why I got all this shit on me," I said just as she opened my fatigue jacket and discovered my pistols. She lightly dropped them on the floor and kicked them down the hall before another chick stepped out of the shadows and picked them up.

She reached around my waist and took the serrated knife off my hip. "Damn, you bought all of this just to be prepared for Rayjon? You sure you ain't bring this stuff to get at me wit'?" She raised her eyebrow and looked up at me from her squatted position.

I shook my head. "I would never hurt you under no circumstances. You know that shit ain't in me to hurt no female."

She stood up wit' the knife in her hand before giving it to the female who had the .9 millimeter pressed to my chest. "I wanna believe you, Racine, but I been in the game long enough to know it's cold as ice." She stepped forward and continued to pat me down. After confirming I was out of weapons, she took a step back. "Look, y'all stand off in the distance, and if anything, look funny, you already know what to do. I gotta have me some of him. Understood?"

I saw the women nod as Averie took my hand and led me into the living room where there was a big queen size bed set up with white sheets and big pillows. All around it were burning jasmine-scented candles. When we were right in front of the bed she walked up to me and kissed my lips real sensuously before sucking on them with her eyes closed. Then she broke the kiss and looked up at me. "Look, Racine, I know we need to talk, and we will, but for right now I need for you to do my pussy like only you can. I need these walls beat in on some savage shit. Can you handle that for me, baby? Huh?" She reached between us and grabbed my dick, then slid her hand into my Gucci pants wrapping her hands around my hot meat before squeezing it again.

I closed my eyes and opened them back up. The feeling was good. As hard as I thought it would have been to go there mentally wit' her, it turned out it wasn't that hard at all. All she needed to do was drop that robe and let me see the body that drove me crazy. At the sight of her round, pretty titties, thick thighs, the li'l pooch of a stomach, and seeing the way her panties were all up in her sex lips, that was all it took. I snapped and figured I might as well enjoy her body, especially if it was going to be the last time.

I picked her up and threw her on the bed, kneeling on the side of her and ripping her panties away from her pussy roughly like I was getting ready to take her pussy, and I honestly was in my mind. I knew what she needed.

"Uh! Shit, Racine! Take this pussy, baby boy. You know what I need!" She opened her legs wide.

I grabbed her by the throat and choked her wit' one hand, leaned down, and sucked on her hard, exposed right nipple. "Bitch, shut up and beg me to not fuck you until you bleed." I sucked her nipple hard while my other hand played between her legs, opening her sex lips and fingering her real hard and fast. I switched from one nipple to the next, sucking wit' all of my might. She loved that rough shit.

"Mm! Mm! Mm! Mm! Uh! Shit, Racine! Take this pussy! Stop playin' wit' me and take my pussy. I need that young dick!" She humped into my fingers as I added a third one and really got to stretching her li'l hole wider.

"Shut up and open them legs wider. Open yo' muthafuckin' legs so I can get in between them better! Now!"

She popped them all the way open. "Uh! Fuck me! Please, baby boy! Fuck me now! I am begging you!"

I jumped between her legs wit' my dick already hard and out of my boxers. Pushing her knees to her chest and choking her wit' my right hand, I slammed my dick into her and got to fucking her so hard I could barely breathe because I was going so fast, making sure I was giving her all of me. And that pussy was good, too. Real wet and meaty.

"Mm! Mm! Mm! Mm! Fuck me! Fuck me, baby boy! Uh! Uh! Uh! Shit! Shit! Yes! Shit! Harder, baby! Ack! Ack! Uh! Ack!"

I choked her harder and got to pounding her out like my life was depending on it, digging as far into her as I could reach with her walls sucking at me and pulling me into her body even more. Our skins slapped together.

She opened her mouth wide and moaned at the top of her lungs. "Uh, shit! You fuckin'. Me. So. Hard. Racine!"

In and out. In and out. In and out. My dick continued to shoot in and out of her pussy at a hundred miles an hour while she dug her nails into my lower waist, scratching me up, but I didn't care.

"I'm cumming, Racine! Baby boy! Uh. I'm cumming! I'm cumming, baby! Just keep killing me! Uh!" she screamed.

Bam. Bam. Bam. Bam. Bam. Bam. Bam. Bam. Bam. Bam. I was long-stroking that pussy and sucking on her neck at the same time wit' her knees pushed to her chest. She was in a li'l ball and couldn't do nothin' but accept my pipe repeatedly.

Afterward, I flipped onto my back and she bounced up and down on my dick like it was a pogo stick. Her titties bounced on her chest, both nipples super hard. Sweat formed on her forehead, but that didn't stop her from riding me like she was trying to break my pipe off inside of her. All the while I rubbed all over that big booty, squeezing it and opening it up.

She continued to ride me while sucking on her bottom lip. "My ass, Racine. Please. I want. You. To. Fuck this ass. Please! Uh!" She screamed and came again on my dick. This time I sat up and sucked on her nipples as she was cumming, holding onto her ass, making her ride me harder. I had already cum deep inside of her pussy.

She jumped off my dick and bent over the bed, opening her thick ass cheeks wide. "Fuck me here, Racine. I want you to fuck me back there like you did before wit' that young dick. Hurry up, baby." She sounded out of breath.

I didn't waste no time getting behind her. I took my pipe and slid it into her pussy to get it nice and soaked from her juices, then slowly guided him into her ass while I took my left hand and played wit' her clitoris.

She moved my fingers out of the way. "I'll do that, baby. I'll do that. Just fuck momma. Use me, baby. Hard!"

I took her hips and pulled her all the way back to me, implanting my dick deep within her butt. The fit was so tight I was ready to cum before I even got going. "Damn, this shit so tight, Averie. I ain't gon' be able to last that long." I pulled out and slammed back into her.

"Uh! Yes! It's okay, li'l daddy! Just fuck. Uh! Just. Just. Uh! Fuck me! As. Long. As you can! Mm!"

She threw her ass back into me while I went on a rampage wit' my eyes pinned on the way her cheeks jiggled and shook. There was nothin' like fucking a thick-ass woman, especially if she gave you access to her whole body.

I fucked her in the back door for the next ten minutes at full speed until I came deep within her, then she laid me on the bed and rode me reverse cowgirl-style with my dick going in and out of her ass while she played wit' her pussy wit' me watching, cumming again and again. That vet sex was the best.

T.J. EDWARDS

Chapter 9

"So, basically, what I'm saying is Rayjon got mad enemies, too. He got killas out in Jersey that want him dead. Killas that are looking for him because of what his father Greed did to them. If you can plug wit' them niggaz and set him up, then they can handle this bitness for us. The only thing is getting your daughter back in one piece before it all goes down." She handed me a blunt and I took it, inhaling deeply fresh out the shower.

I adjusted her a li'l bit in my lap, making sure her fat booty was right in my center. I had a li'l thing for Averie. I can't even lie about that. After we'd got done fucking, I kept shit one-hunnit wit' her and told her what Rayjon expected of me. I know most people might have thought that was a dumb move, but at the same time I knew Averie wasn't a dumb female. If she had chosen to break his ass off in the beginning just to give everything to me, I felt like she deserved some type of loyalty from me. Besides, pillow talk was a muthafucka. She had been with Rayjon for a long time. She knew him better than anybody else. That nigga stayed running his mouth to her about everything when they were together, so she knew him inside and out. His strengths, his weaknesses, all of it. She never denied he was a goon, but at the same time she just didn't feel he could out-think both of us, and I agreed one-hunnit percent.

I inhaled the weed smoke and held it in my lungs for a few seconds before blowing it back out. I held her more firmly to me. "What are the odds you can get me and them niggaz to have a sit-down? I'm talking, like, within the next few days, too."

She got off my lap naked. Her titties wobbling on her chest as she leaned down and received the blunt from me. I couldn't help looking between her thick thighs, peeping that fat kat tucked there. Averie had one of them custom-made million-dollar stripper bodies. I loved it. That's why every time I got on top of her ass I tore that shit up.

She licked her juicy lips, then took a pull off the blunt. "I'll do my part. You just be waiting for my call. And in the meantime, keep playin' ball wit' him. And don't worry, you ain't gon' have to do it for much longer."

I stood up and slipped into my Gucci pants. "And what about yo' head? That nigga saying he want yo' shit, like, right away. What we gon' do about that?"

She scrunched her face, then curled her upper lip. "Rayjon so pussy to me. How that nigga gon' call fo' my head like he straight up savage like his father Greed? Now, that was a goon if I ever saw one. He just trying his best to be like him, but I never heard of Greed taking nobody's little daughter, though. That's fucked up." She took another pull off the blunt and handed it back to me. "I'ma hit you up tomorrow, and I'll have a head for you and some connects that's real important. Until then you just keep playin' the game Rayjon about to lose."

She took a deep breath, then exhaled slowly, walking up to me and standing on her tippy-toes so she could kiss my lips with her eyes closed. After the peck, she took a step back and smiled up at me, placing her arms around my waist. "Racine, I know we done got ourselves into a bunch of bullshit, but I just want you to know I got you. I will not let this nigga defeat you or hurt your daughter. You have my word. I'm going to do everything in my power, so we prevail. I care about you, baby boy." She reached up and stroked my cheek with the back of her fingers. "You're so pure. You are meant to be a boss, and I'm gon' help you get there. I promise." She looked into my eyes, then hugged me, laying her head on my chest.

After I left Averie's duck-off crib, I made it no further than two blocks away from the highway when E and Wayne pulled up on me in an all-black van. They pulled to my driver's side, and Wayne was in the passenger's seat of their probably-stolen van. Wayne waved to me and told me to pullover, which I did. I got out and walked up to their van and looked through his passenger's window and saw an all black twelve-gauge on his lap. He had on black leather gloves as well. E Had a mini-hatchet on his lap. He also wore black gloves.

"Bruh, so what's happening? We finna go back and cut that bitch's head off, or what?" Wayne asked, tightening his gloves on his hand.

"Yeah, bruh, you had us waiting out here all night like we was finna get in shorty an' 'em ass. Then I creep up to the window and see you in there fucking her brains out. I'm confused as hell right now. So, tell me what the move gon' be?" E said, rubbing the side of the hatchet's blade with a frown on his face.

I shook my head. "Nall, she working on somethin' for me that should help us out a lot. So, for right now she get a pass until I see where she going wit' things." I didn't want to tell them too much because I was still trying to piece together everything she had told me she was going to do. I felt like the less they knew for now, the better off we would be, at least until I saw how Averie handled what she told me she would.

Wayne shrugged his shoulders. "A'ight then. If we ain't hitting her up right now, then we gotta get to the Taylors. My li'l niggaz been rocking the trap. We got about two-hunnit stacks we gotta snatch up. After we get that paper, we gotta hit up a few Mickey Cobra niggaz that's off State. They making it seem like they wanna make a play for our buildings, and I know it's because we ain't physically been there to show the hood it's our turf now. So, we gotta splash these kats and then spend some time in the Projects. That fool Tez already on his way there. Oh, and later tonight we riding out to Milwaukee so we can hit this lick. Guaranteed no less than five-hunnit bands, not counting the dope."

My eyes got bucked as hell because I was already calculating that total. He was saying we had two-hunnit stacks to snatch up from the Projects, and then the lick out in Milwaukee would give us no less than five-hunnit gees, not including the dope and whatever else. That was seven-hunnit bands right there, which meant I was only three-hunnit short. I was all for that.

The only thing that was throwing me off was Rayjon said he was going to have me hit up some mo' niggaz, and I didn't know when he wanted me to do it. Long as it didn't conflict wit' what we had going on, I felt like everything would be a success.

"Look, Wayne, y'all already know that nigga expecting me to come up wit' another mill by the end of next week. Now, this paper you saying we got coming add up to seven-hunnit bands. You niggaz gon' let me get all of this for my daughter's ransom, or what?"

Wayne scrunched his face and looked me up and down. "Without a muthafuckin' question, ma nigga. Every lick we hit until she back in yo' arms go toward getting her back. This loyalty is real. You ain't never gotta ask me no shit like that no mo'."

E continued to rub the blade of the hatchet. "The sooner we get her back and kill that nigga, the sooner we can get back to cartel bitness. You ain't in this shit alone. We'll eat when you really eat. For now, we working for yo' seed, big homie. This loyalty in blood. Now, let's fuck some shit up until we get you right."

Hearing this come from my dudes made my heart beat faster. I could honestly say I loved these niggaz, and I would make sure that after it was all said and done, they became rich men under me. I would make sure their families were well taken care of for years and years to come. I didn't know how I was going to make all of it happen, I just knew I was. It was in me to be a boss. I knew once I got halfway right I would make sure my crew was eating so much they constantly burped.

I stuck my head all the way in the window and gave that fool Wayne a half-hug. "I love you, bruh, and my loyalty is in blood for you and yours."

He hugged me back. "I already know, big homie. That's why I'm riding wit' you until my last breath, the Ski Mask way. Blood in, blood out, ma nigga."

E got out of the van, came around the front of it, and gave me a half-hug. "I love you too, big homie, and I got you for life, ma nigga. Trust my gangsta." He hugged me tight.

I hugged him back. "I love you too, homie, and I'll meet that Reaper wit' you any day of the week. Trust and believe that."

An hour later we were pulling up into the parking lot of the Robert Taylor Home projects that we'd taken over from J-Rock and his crew of Murda Mafia BDs. It was about one in the morning, and I would think everybody would have been inside of their cribs, but instead when we pulled up we were met by about twenty dudes with their hats broke off to the left, indicating they were under the five-point star.

I jumped out of my truck, and Wayne and E got out of their van and stood on the side of me, one man on each arm. The crew we were looking at seemed to bind together, mugging us like they had some bullshit on their minds.

I stepped forward. "What you niggaz doing in our parking lot, homie? The Taylors under new management. Y'all gotta step."

Some fat nigga with some long-ass dreads and a five-point star under his left eye stepped forward with a scowl on his face. "Man, you don't' tell my niggaz where the fuck they gotta go. This our hood. J-Rock gone, so that mean us Mickey Cobras taking over," he said, sounding like Kodak Black.

I ain't like this nigga. He must have thought it was sweet wit' us or something. I scrunched my face and stepped closer to him. His niggaz put their hands under their shirts like they were ready to air us out. "Who is you, homie?"

He laughed real briefly, then looked over his shoulder at his men. "I'm Choppah, and I'm chief of the Cobras. This our building now, so we ain't gotta go nowhere. You got that, nigga?"

He looked me up and down as a few more kats came out of the building and stood off in the distance, just watching the scene unfold. In Chicago the worst thing that could happen to a nigga when he was trying to build a mob was to let onlookers see him be hoed-out by the chief or a member of another gang. He would never be able to live that down. At that moment I was standing face-to-face with the next crew that felt like they were in line to take over a building that grossed over five-hunnit gees a day from narcotics. A building me and my crew had murdered multiple niggaz to get. I couldn't go out like that. I had to exercise my gangsta.

Before this muthafucka could make another move, I whipped both .9 millimeters out of my holsters and put both barrels to each of his eyes and cocked the hammers on them. "Bitch-nigga, fuck you, and fuck them Cobras. My name is Racine, and I'm chief of the Ski Mask Cartel, and this building, along wit' this ward, belongs to us!" I hollered this shit in his ear as loud as I could.

Behind him, his guys pulled out their guns. Out of the twenty kats, only about ten pistols were pulled out. I wanted to laugh at that because what type of chief was he if he couldn't even arm his whole crew?

He threw his arms in the air just as Wayne and E upped their weapons, E wit' two Mach .90s and Wayne wit' two Uzis. All four weapons had extended clips and were more than capable of killing everybody out there.

"Racine, say the word and we'll leave every muthafucka out here in blood. This our shit. Ski Mask Cartel, bitch-niggaz!" Wayne hollered at the top of his lungs.

He lowered his eyes into slits. "Y'all muthafuckas don't want no war, Jo, I swear. Everybody gon' die. I'm just telling you now, that's on my son!"

"Everybody die, then!" said some skinny li'l nigga holding a .38 special. I knew he only had six shots in that weak-ass gun, and even though it could do some damage, I was sure I would have knocked his head off before he was able to do anything.

I forced the barrels of my guns into Choppah's eyes even harder. "Tell yo' li'l nigga to stand down. Now!" I hollered, ready to push his shit back. "Tell him!"

"A'ight! A'ight! Yo, Blue, go sit yo' ass down before you get me killed. I ain't on that shit tonight, man. This some bullshit."

Blue bugged his eyes. "What! Are you fuckin' kidding me?" He lowered his gun and put it back under his shirt, shaking his head the whole time as if he couldn't believe how Choppah was getting down.

Just then Tez came out of the shadows with seven young niggaz behind him holding our AR-15s Ellie had got for us. "Like the homie said, you niggaz don't want no war wit' us. We killing everything and everybody." He aimed his assault rifle at their crew, and so did the young killas behind him.

I noted another crew came out of the buildings and stood off in the distance. They were Vice Lords and looked to be about fifteen deep. I decided to use this moment as an opportunity. I knew the Vice Lords also rode under the five-point star, which meant they were somehow or another aligned wit' the Mickey Cobras we had at gunpoint. Instead of beefing wit' both of their mobs, I decided to take a different approach.

"Look, the Taylors under new management, but I ain't on no greedy shit. I wanna make sure everybody that's from this land is eating real good. Ain't no way we should be out here beefing when its so much money to be made all across the board. I'm open to sittin down with the Cobras and you Lords over there. If y'all will give me your ear, I'll show you how we can all get rich together and work in harmony."

Everybody was quiet for a long time, then a tall, lanky kat from the crew of Lords walked over to us with his gang only a few feet behind him. When he got close enough, he held up a hand.

"Look, muthafuckas can't be out here beefing and making money at the same time. Something gotta give. I got about fifty niggaz that ride under me. If you saying you got a way I can keep feeding my niggaz and avoid beefing wit' your cartel, then I'm all ears. I heard how that fool J-Rock ended up. I ain't got time fo' that shit. I'm trying to eat in these streets. The Taylors is a gold mine." He waved his crew over. "Let me hear what's on yo' mind?"

"What you gotta say, Choppah, huh?" I asked, pressing the gun harder into his face now.

Boom! His brains splashed all over my Gucci fit and even got into my mouth, scaring the shit out of me. I jumped back and got ready to let my .9s ride when I looked up and saw Blue standing over him with a smoking gun.

Boom! Boom! Boom! Boom! Boom! Choppah's body leaped on the pavement again and again. Then Blue stepped over his leaking form. "Fuck that nigga. He ain't got no heart. I'm calling for the Mickey Cobras now. Any of my niggaz got a problem wit' that?" he asked, looking over his crew.

They shook their heads and continued to look down on Choppah's dead body. I would learn later that Choppah was Blue's big brother. Blue didn't have no heart. He came to be one of my hitters I relied on in this cartel.

That night we spent two hours getting an understanding. The Lords wanted to be free to move their coke through the Taylor buildings, while the Mickey Cobras didn't have a set drug they wanted to push because they were basically stick-up men. So, me and Tez decided we would use them to both push our heroin and hit licks when we needed them to. It turned out to be about forty of them altogether in that ward, so Tez arranged for a sit-down so we could get an understanding wit' them and our cartel.

All I cared about was the Taylors was still ours. We were the controlling body of the buildings, and now that we didn't have to worry about any rival crews in the area, the cartel was free to make as much money as possible. I intended to capitalize off that.

After picking up two-hunnit and fifty thousand dollas from the li'l homies we let run the trap, me, Wayne, and E was headed out to Milwaukee, so we could hit that five-hunnit-thousand dolla lick that had me salivating at the mouth. I didn't know much about Milwaukee, but from what Wayne and E was telling me on the way, there was plenty of money out there in that city. Money, we needed to get our hands on by any and every means.

T.J. EDWARDS

Chapter 10

"A'ight, Racine, they call this the Cheetah Club. Now, when we get inside, it's gon' look like a normal strip club, but that's just a front. I got a li'l eighteen-year-old bitch that work in here. She fucking the owner, a nigga named Big Tim. Now, word to me was this nigga serve boatloads of heroin all over Milwaukee and the rest of Wisconsin. He was knee-deep in the game way before he opened this ratchet-ass strip club. Now, she say the nigga done downed her plenty times in his office. He got a safe in the floor right under his desk. He in love wit' my li'l bitch's pussy, so much so he done opened the safe a bunch of times in front of her. So much so she know the combination by heart."

I nodded as E continued to drive on the highway and eat a burrito at the same time. "A'ight, that sound cool. But how you know for a fact it got over five-hunnit gees inside of it? I mean, she can't eyeball money like that, can she?"

Wayne nodded his head and put a few french fries into his mouth before chewing them up and swallowing. "Nall, but you see, this tricking-ass nigga got a habit of jacking to her. He crazy on that pillow talk shit, too. She say after they get done fucking, all that nigga do is run his mouth about everything, which is why after we hit this safe in his club we taking him to his crib out in West Allis and emptying that safe, too. It's supposed to be filled up wit' heroin. We need all that shit. You feel me?" He took a burrito out of the bag, turned his head to the side, and bit into it with his eyes closed.

I bit into my Reuben sandwich, and it was so good I just had to take a moment to appreciate its taste. Mm. "A'ight. So, look, Wayne, since this yo' lick, I'ma let you run point on this one, and me and E just gon' follow yo' lead. Keep in mind we don't know shit about this city, so we outta bounds and vulnerable as hell."

He swallowed the food he had in his mouth and washed it down with the grape pop he'd bought. "Bruh, y'all my niggaz. I would never bring y'all way out here if I didn't have everything under control. I know this city like the back of my hand. All my cousins trap through 45th, and they wrecking shit. I been up here more than enough times to know everything that's going on. Just follow my lead and trust me. Oh, and after we rob this nigga, we gotta kill him and my li'l bitch. I just can't take the risk he ain't gone put two and two together, and on her side, I can't risk her not opening her mouth about this li'l move. So, it is what it is."

I shrugged my shoulders. "Look, like I said, you running point. Whatever you want us to do, we'll do it."

"That's all I ask," Wayne said, eating some more of his french fries.

The Cheetah Club was a rundown-ass strip club that looked ghetto as hell. I wouldn't have let any one of them females walking around inside that muthafucka sit on my lap. First, they all looked rundown and like all they did all day long was pills and dope. Most of them were real skinny sistas, while others were a little too thick to have their shirts off trying to make money. I mean, some of these sistas had stomachs hanging all over their waists, and their panties were way too small for 'em, and not in a good way.

We came through the door and paid the ten-dollar cover charge, then was escorted by a halfway-decent-looking dark-skinned sista wit' red hair. She led us to a table all the way in the back of the club. It smelled like musk and cigarette smoke inside of it. I looked around and noted that besides us, there were about fifteen other people. Mostly older dudes, too. They were getting lap dances while Cardi B rapped out of the speakers.

The club had one main stage that currently had a chubby female dancer trying to put it together. She really didn't look like she knew how to dance, but I guessed she was trying her best to figure it out. I simply shook my head.

"Bruh, these broads popped as hell in here. I feel sicker on the stomach than anything."

Wayne curled his upper lip. "I wouldn't touch any one of these bitchez in here wit' yo' dick, my nigga. These hoez famous for burning kats. We ain't finna be in here for too long. Just gotta wait for Toya to come from the back."

E smiled. "You niggaz tripping. You see all these big girls in here? I feel like I'm in fat ho heaven." E continued to watch the chubby chick on stage do her best to twerk. I peeped it for a second and honestly felt sick. I ain't have no problems wit' big girls, but shorty on stage just wasn't doing it for me. I think it was because she was sweating way too much, and I could see her track coming out of her hair. I knew E loved all kinds of big girls, though, but mainly white ones.

We sat there for about ten minutes when Toya came from the back and walked up to the table. She was a li'l, short, caramel female, thick, with a real pretty face. I didn't understand how she could be dancing at that club because, judging by the look of the other females, she didn't fit in. I figured she must've been taking all their money, easily.

She came and sat on Wayne's lap. "Hey, daddy, I see you finally made it out here. I'm so happy, too, because that nigga back there leaning hard as hell off four Perc-30s."

I knew she was talking about Percocet-30s. I never really got into that pill game, but I understood the lingo.

Wayne scrunched his face, and I saw him grab a handful of her thigh roughly. "Look, everything you told me better be one-hunnit. You know I don't play about my money. Now I got my niggaz wit' me, and we looking to bust this move, so g'on back there and get shit situated. Text me that you love me when it's time for me to come through that office do'. You understand that?"

She winced in pain, then nodded her head. "But I do love you, Wayne, and I'ma make sure you get everything from this nigga I said you would. I'll do anything for you." Her eyes got watery, then she swallowed her spit.

He nodded his head and made her get off his lap, her thong riding high in her ass crack. "Shorty, actions speak louder than words. Let's handle this bitness, then I'll determine if you love me or not, or what you will and won't do for me. G'on, and hit my phone wit' that text when it's time."

I wanted to tell the homie he was handling her kinda rough, but I decided against it. This was his mission, and we were close to getting five-hunnit stacks, so if handling her like that was how he got us to this point, who was I to judge his ways toward his women?

"That's fucked up. Toya look like she the only decent one in this bitch. She ain't got enough meat on her bones for me, though," E said, eyeing the big-boned sista that was just getting off the stage. She must've saw him because she walked right up to our table and stood in front of E, wiping sweat from her face wit' a napkin.

"Excuse me, baby, but I saw you peeping me kind of hard while I was doing my routine up there. You want a private dance?" she asked him, licking her lips.

E smiled and looked over to me, but I looked off. I just wanted to get up out of there. I didn't like the smell of it, I didn't like the women, and I didn't know shit about the city I was in. I wanted us to bust this move and get the fuck back home to Chicago where I understood the slums of my jungle.

E turned to her and looked her up and down. "Maybe I'll catch you before I leave, sweetheart.

I mean, I was feeling how you did yo' thang up there, so just save me a private dance and we'll get better acquainted."

She smiled "Okay, baby, I'll do that. Now enjoy this view as I walk away." She stepped away from our booth and got to switching as hard as she could, I imagined.

"Mm. Mm. Mm!" E said, looking at her flat ass the whole time. I just wanted to get up out of there. I was disgusted.

Wayne's phone buzzed. He looked down at the face and smiled, then he pointed wit' his head toward our left. I saw Toya standing in the hallway that led to the bathrooms and the strippers' locker room. "Yo, it's time. Let's go get this money, my niggaz."

I reached into my pants and yanked the taped Glock from my thigh while my homies did the same thing. Had the club not been so dimly lit, I'm sure people would have noticed us with our hands down our pants. But as far as I knew they didn't, and in a matter of second we were up and following Toya down the hallway, past the bathrooms, and through the fire escape.

Once out back, we took the stairs down a flight and stopped in front of a wall that had a fire extinguisher on it. She reached into the case and pushed the extinguisher in, and the wall popped out. She pulled on it, and it opened wide enough for us to slip through it. We wound up in another hallway that was covered in white carpet.

I tightened my grip on my pistol, and about ten steps inside the hallway I cocked it back, ready to handle this bitness. Like I said before, I had never been to this city, so I didn't know how these kats got down up here. True enough, I was letting Wayne run point on this mission, but at the same time I had be on point just for my own psyche and the welfare of my dudes.

As we walked down the hallway, I noted the walls were lined with various paintings of old famous pimps. To my left, E cocked back his pistol. Wayne saw him and did the same thing. The short hallway ended in front of a closed door that had the word "Daddy" written across it in big, bold gold lettering.

Toya turned around and faced us with a finger up to her lips, then she pointed and directed us to stand on the side of the door. Once we had, she fixed her hair, took a deep breath, and knocked on the door.

"Who is it?" came a deep voice from the other side of it.

She exhaled loudly and fixed her bra over her titties, then pulled her G-string further up her round ass before popping back on her legs. "It's me, Daddy. I need to talk to you real fast before I go out and handle my set."

There was a brief silence. I lowered my eyes and felt my heartbeat speed up. My adrenalin got to coursing through me, and I was ready for action.

I heard a lock turn on the door, and then it opened to reveal of big, black, fat-ass nigga with no shirt on. He appeared to be sweating and everything while his chest heaved up and down.

He looked down on Toya with a mug on his face. "Damn, girl, what you want? We in here on somethin' right now," he hollered into her face, and I could tell he was irritated.

"Well, I just wanted to tell Tim that –"

That was as far as she got before I moved her out of the way and slammed the handle of my pistol into this big nigga's forehead, hitting his ass hard enough to knock him backward. Wham! "Bitch-ass nigga, get the fuck out of the way!" I hollered and rushed into the office while he put both of his big hands over his face. I caught him again with the pistol, this time on the side of his temple since his hands were covering his face.

"Uh!" He threw his hands into the air and fell face-first to the floor. It was then I noticed all he had on was a pair of boxers.

Big Tim got ready to jump out of his office chair when E ran in the room at full speed and yanked him across it, knocking his lap top on the floor along with a whole bunch of other things. He slung him to the ground and pressed the barrel of his gun to his forehead. "Bitch-ass nigga, where the safe at?"

Wayne brought Toya into the room and threw her over by me. "And don't lie, neither, because she already told us everything. Yo' best bet is to open that muthafucka and let us be on our merry way or shit finna get real bloody in this bitch."

Tim shook his head from side to side. "I ain't got no safe, man. That bitch lying. I ain't got no money in here at all. What, do you think I'm stupid or somethin'?" He tried to sit up and E forced him back to the ground. His silk robe opened just enough to let us all know he was naked underneath it. I didn't know what him and that big nigga was doing before we showed up, but I definitely had my suspicions. I understood now why the big dude was so irritated. All I could do was shake my head.

E smacked him across the face with his pistol. *Wham!* Then he choked him for ten seconds before taking his hands from around his neck. "This shit ain't a game, ma nigga. Now, I'm gon' tell you one last time. Get yo' punk-ass up and lead me to the safe."

Blood oozed out of Tim's nose and mouth. He had a huge gash right where his cheek and the left side of his nose met. "I ain't got no money here, man. I would never have no cash in this club. I know where I'm at." He whimpered, sounding out of breath.

Toya walked over to him and looked down at his bleeding face. "You lying, Tim. You got a safe right under this desk, and the combination is your daughter's birthdate. You trying to get me killed, but I don't need you." She kicked him in the ribs and he blew out a puff of air. "Y'all move this desk. The safe right under there, and I'll open it up," she said, looking from Wayne down to E

I didn't wait for neither one of my li'l homies to move. I pushed the desk all the way against the wall. I didn't care of it was oak or not. I wanted to get up out of there and that city, period. I didn't know how long it would be before somebody checked on him to make sure he was straight, and the way Wayne was talking, we still had to take him out to his crib in West Allis to retrieve the dope he had hidden there. I was already deciding against that. It just seemed too risky for an out-of-town lick.

As soon as the desk was moved out of the way, Toya dropped to her knees and pulled the red carpet back, exposed the face of the safe inside of the floor. "I told you that nigga was lying," she said, opening the control panel. "You done forced yourself on me too many times in this office for me to not know where everything is. Fucking pervert. You and his gay-ass," she said, looking down at the fat nigga I'd put to sleep.

E started to choke Tim again while he kicked his legs up under him. "Ack! Hack! Ah! Ack!" Tighter and tighter E squeezed with his eyes lowered into slits.

Wayne leaned down and tapped him on the shoulder. "Wait, bruh. Let's make sure she got the actual combination before you body his ass."

Toya was busy punching away on the keypad. She looked like she was in a hurry. She punched in the numbers and pressed pound, but the face of the screen kept on flashing red. She bugged her eyes. "I don't get it. I know it's his daughter's birthday. I watched him punch it in not more than two hours ago when Casey brought him ten thousand dollars. I must be doing somethin' wrong," she said, looking like she was ready to freak out. She started to punch on the keypad all over again.

I ain't have no time for that shit. We had to get up out of there. I reached down and grabbed one of Tim's hands, took a finger, and broke it sideways.

"Aw! Aw! You muthafucka! You!" Tim hollered with his mouth wide open.

Wham! E smacked him with his pistol again, this time so hard he spit three teeth. They fell onto his lip before dropping to the floor in a puddle of blood.

"Bitch-ass nigga, what's the combination? Now! Last chance," E growled and cocked back the hammer on his pistol, forcing it down Tim's throat so far he started to gag over it.

"Argh! Argh! I, argh!" He sounded like he was drowning in water, kicking his legs, now exposing his nakedness.

"You gon' tell us the combo, nigga? Huh? You gon' tell us what we want to hear? You done playing?" E asked, forcing the gun further down his throat. Tim gagged and threw up over the barrel, but that didn't stop E from forcing it further down.

Tim nodded his head. "Argh! Arr!" E pulled the gun out of his mouth. "A'ight, man. She gotta hit the pound sign three times before she punch in my daughter's birthdate, then hit it another three times after she punches it in. She do that and it's gon' open up. Y'all take the money and go. I don't want no problems wit' you niggaz," he said before throwing up a little more on his chest. It smelled like he'd been eating hotdogs or somethin'.

127

Toya was already doing what he'd said. "I told you one day karma was gon' get yo' ass, Tim. You done raped every girl in this club. Now you getting what you deserve." She finished punching in the code and the safe started to beep repeatedly before it popped open. "Hell yeah!" she hollered, then stood up and looked up at Wayne. "That bitch filled, daddy, and it's all yours."

Wayne bumped her out of the way slightly, and I peeped how sick she looked. I knelt down in front of the safe wit' him and saw it was filled to the max with stacks and stacks of money. We took the bags out of our underwear and got to filling them up with the cash.

"Y'all can let me go now, man. I ain't gon' call the police. I got got. That's a part of the game," Tim said trying to sit up.

I shook my head. "Nall, nigga, it's curtains. "E, kill that nigga. We ain't fucking wit' that other lick. We gotta get back to the land. We'll make up for that dope."

Wayne mugged me. "Damn, when you figure all this out?" he said, shoving more and more money into the bag. "I thought Milwaukee was my thing?"

"Just gotta go wit' my gut on this one, bruh. Don't worry, I see how you trying to handle bitness for our crew. You gon' have plenty time to lead while we follow, just now ain't that time. You understand that?" I said, taking out the last few bundles and putting them in my bag.

He shrugged his shoulders. "A'ight, you chief, so let's ride, then. E, kill that nigga, and I'll take care of Toya." He stood up and grabbed her by the shirt, putting his gun to her forehead.

She shook her head. "Wayne, what are you doing? Please don't. I thought I was showing you how much I cared about you by putting you up on this money." She blinked tears and started to shake.

Wayne sucked his teeth. "Shorty, I can't trust you like that. You done seen my niggaz's face, and you know me. The rules of the street say you gotta go, so that's what it is." He pushed her against the wall by her neck and put the pistol to her forehead.

"Please, no! Wayne! I'm pregnant wit' yo' child! Don't kill us!" she screamed and winced as if he'd already pulled the trigger.

E had his forearm on Tim's neck, holding him to the floor with his teeth clenched. Tim tried to struggle against him, but it was pointless.

"You what?" Wayne asked, loosening his grip.

She slowly opened her eyes. "I'm pregnant with your child. I was gon' tell you that before all of this, but I didn't find a window to. Please don't kill me. I'm begging you."

I watched Wayne shake his head, and as crazy as it may sound, I felt sorry for Toya. I understood the game said she was supposed to die, but after hearing how Tim had raped her multiple times and how stomp-down she was for Wayne, I just felt like I needed to step in. "Toya, you supposed to be dead, ma, because you know too much. But I'll tell you what, if you kill both niggaz, we gon' let you live."

Wayne mugged me. "What? Nigga, hell nall." He put the pistol back to her forehead.

I ran over and pulled his arm away. "Nigga, hold up. Now, she might be carrying yo' seed, fo' real. I know how you get down for yo' daughter back home. I know you'd never kill yo' own kid, man. Think about it." I didn't know why I was sticking my neck out for her like that because I didn't even know her. I guess I was just looking at how big Tim and Casey was, and I imagined them raping her all the time, and that made me feel sorry for her. I didn't know if she really had the homie's seed growing in her or not, but I didn't want us to kill her. "Now, if she kill them, that makes us all even. Let her handle this bitness."

Wayne held her against the wall for a moment, then let her go. "I got love for you, Toya, but you betta not be lying about what's inside of you. Kill these bitch-niggaz, and me and you gon' get an understanding." He handed her the gun and stepped to the side.

Chapter 11

Toya knelt alongside E while he held his forearm on Tim's neck. She blinked tears, then wiped them away. "I hate you, Tim. I always hated you. Every time you forced yourself on me, you killed me inside. Nobody deserves that!"

She put the barrel of Wayne's gun to his left eye and pulled the trigger. *Boom!* His head leaped off the floor. Blood spurted from the side of his head, but he was still moving and trying to talk. E stood up in amazement, looking down on him.

"Uh! Uh! B-ah!" He turned to his side and I was able to see the massive hole in the side of his head. Half of his face was blown off.

"Shoot his bitch-ass again, Toya. Hurry up!" Wayne ordered.

She aimed the gun downward and busted. *Boom! Boom!* "Die, Tim! I hate you!"

Both bullets slammed into the back of his head, causing it to explode. Tim fell onto his stomach, unmoving. Toya looked down on him with her eyes wide open as if she could not believe what she'd just done. I noticed her arms shaking, and her upper lip twitching while she held the pistol with both hands, still aimed down at Tim.

"Come on, shorty. You got one more to go. Body his ass, too," I said, nodding wit' my head at Casey's fat ass. He was still knocked out cold with his eyes closed.

Toya walked over to him and aimed the gun directly at his face, before closing her eyes. *Boom! Boom! Boom!* "Ah!" She took a step back with the smoking gun, looking down at Casey's holey body. His brains leaked out of the side of his head and oozed along his shoulder.

Wayne stepped forward and grabbed his gun from her. "Look, big homie, y'all head back to the land, and I'll meet y'all back there in a day or so. Me and her gotta get an understandin'. I love you niggaz, fo' real." He handed his bag of money to E, and gave me half a hug before doing the same thing to E

Toya ran up and hugged me while he was hugging E. "Thank you for saving my life. I owe you," she whispered into my ear.

I didn't know what Wayne had in mind, but me and E got up out of there and let him finish up that lick.

***

When I got home that night, Tez was already at my crib. I came in through the backdoor because I had all that blood and shit on my clothes. I heard a male voice coming from the living room, followed by Kenosha giggling. *I know damn well this broad don't got no nigga in my crib.* I knew better than that.

I whipped out my banger, dropped the money on the floor, and made my way toward the front of the house with murder on my mind.

When I got closer, I recognized the voice of my cousin, Tez. Although that knowledge calmed my suspicions, it did nothing to lower my temper.

The fact of the matter was she had a nigga in my house in my absence. I didn't play that shit.

Upon entering the living room, they looked up at me like deer caught in headlights.

"Hey, baby. What's wrong? Why you lookin' at me like that?' Kenosha asked.

"What the fuck you mean, what's wrong? You sittin' up here with a nigga in my living room wearing some see-through shit. I can see your nipples and everything."

Tez scrunched his face. "Wait a minute, cuz, what you trying to say?" He took a step toward me.

I flared my nostrils and clenched my jaw. "Tez, on some real shit, cuz, you ain't supposed to be in here holding my baby mother while I ain't here. I never crossed that line wit' Raven like that because I knew better, and you should, too."

Kenosha lowered her head. "Well damn, Racine, I been in here breaking down and going through it for the last few days. I feel like I'm losing myself, and you ain't tryin' to see that. I need somebody here to console me right now because I don't know what to do. Tez was my only safe option because I know you don't want some other nigga all up in this house," she said, sniffling.

I curled my upper lip. "I don't want no nigga in here while I'm not here. And once again, look how you dressed. You pregnant, and you parading around in front of my cousin like he me or something. That shit ain't cool."

Tez waved me off. "Cuz, I don't even look at her like that. You tripping. Look, I'm 'bout to get up out of here and let y'all talk or whatever y'all gotta do. I ain't mean no disrespect by stepping in for her. I thought you would have appreciated it more than anything else." He picked up his pistol off the table and put it on his hip before walking to the front door and unlocking it. He looked over his shoulder at me. "Bruh, I don't know what's going on wit' you, but you know I would never cross you like that wit' yo' baby momma." He shook his head.

I laughed sarcastically because I was getting more and more heated. "Nigga, you should have told her to go and put some fuckin' clothes on. You ain't even hug up wit' yo' own bitch like that."

Before he could respond, we both turned our heads at the sound of tires screeching and saw guns being drawn.

Boom! Boom! Boom! Boom! Boom! More shots rang out. Pictures were shot off the walls and crashed to the floor. The fish tank shattered, and I saw the little fish that were inside of it flopping around on the carpet.

Boom! Boom! Boom! Boom! Boom! Boom! Boom! Boom! I didn't know who the fuck was busting at us, but they were trying to take our heads off. I thought they were just going to shoot at the front of the house when the side windows exploded. *Doom! Doom! Doom!* Glass splattered all over our bodies, yet I kept Kenosha covered with all of me. If any bullets were going to slam into either one of us, I was hoping it was going to be me. I would die if anything happened to her.

Boo-wa! Boo-wa! Boo-wa! Boo-wa! Tez continued to bust his gun until we heard them squealing away from the curb. I continued to cover Kenosha for another two whole minutes. Once I figured we were out of harm's way, I jumped up and pulled her up along wit' me. "Baby, go in there and get dressed. Hurry up. We getting the fuck outta here. Go!"

Tez ran into the dining room where we were with his gun still smoking. "Them fuck-niggaz shot up my Porsche, man." He frowned and started dialing on his phone.

My brain was spinning like crazy. "Who do you think that was? Was you able to see anybody?" I asked, not knowing what to think or who to go at, and then my phone buzzed, and Rayjon's punk-ass face popped up on the screen.

Tez shook his head. "Nall, all I saw was it was two black vans, and like five niggaz busting at us. I don't know if they saw my whip and got at us or if it was an enemy that knew where you stayed. Either way, my head reeling, cuz."

Mine was, too. I picked up the phone. "What's good, Rayjon?" I took a step away from Tez in the direction of my bedroom. I needed to get dressed and get out of that house. I knew it was only a matter of time before the police would show up asking questions. We stayed in a suburb of Chicago called Riverdale. For the most part it was a decent area, and the police made their presence felt out there, which is why we needed to hurry up and get out of that house. I also stepped away from Tez because I didn't want Rayjon to hear his voice and order me to cut my cousin's head off right there on the spot.

"Look, I got a move for you that gotta be busted between five and six in the morning. I'm sending you the address right now. Make it happen and bring me the money, then take care of everybody inside of the crib." After he said those words, he hung up the phone and the address to the lick came across my phone's screen. I felt sick on the stomach and tired at the same time.

Tez lowered his phone. "Who was that on the phone, cuz?" He looked me over closely.

"That nigga Rayjon. He want me to bust a move for him out in Evanston at five in the morning." I shook my head. "This shit getting crazy."

Tez scrunched his face. "Let's just kill that nigga and get the shit over wit'. I'm pretty sure we can get Madison back at the same time." He put his gun back on his hip and looked over my shoulder.

Kenisha was slipping her coat on, fully dressed now. She walked over to me and laid her head on my chest. "Baby you ready to go?" She wrapped her arm around my lower waist.

I looked over at Tez. "You see, that's the problem, Tez. I can't function with no 'pretty sures' when it comes to my daughter. I'ma find a way to get her back, then that nigga gon' reap what he sowed."

An hour later, Kenosha was sitting on the bed in front of me with her head bowed. I looked down on her in silence. "You know you was out of order, don't you?" I asked, lifting her chin with my fingers so she could look into my eyes.

She blinked a few times, then nodded her head. "Yes, daddy. I do now, but I honestly didn't at the time. I thought I was doing the right thing by calling Tez instead of some other nigga. Like I said before, I am mentally going through it right now, and I need you more than ever. I'm so scared for our daughter and for you. It seems like you going up against some heavy hitters, and I don't know what that actually means for our family, so I'm scared all the time. I just want us to all be together with the new baby somewhere far, far away from Chicago because it ain't nothin' here for us but death."

I took her face into both of my hands and rubbed her cheeks with my thumbs. "I love you so much, baby. I swear to God I do. You know it ain't nothin' in this world I wouldn't do for you. I just wanna make sure you never have to work a day in your life. I wanna make sure our daughter has the best of the best because that's my job. Anything you want and need, you should be able to have with no questions asked." I swallowed. "I appreciate you, Kenosha, with everything that I am, and I don't mean to be so bogus toward you, but you know I'm a street nigga. I gotta go out there and make it happen for us. I can't let us starve, baby. I'd rather die first." I felt my eyes getting misty. I tilted my head back and opened them wide to avoid the tears falling out of them. "I fucked up, Kenosha, but I gotta figure this shit out, baby. I can't let us lose. I can't let our family be defeated like this." I blinked, and the tears came pouring out of my eyes. I didn't even care no more.

Kenosha stood up on her tippy-toes, kissing my lips. "Baby, I already know you have our family on your back and you just want to make sure we have everything we need. I have never doubted you. Not even right now while we're under fire." She stepped on her tippy-toes again and kissed my lips. "I know you'll figure this out, daddy. I know you're going to get our daughter back home safe and make Rayjon pay for his sins. He can never get away with this. I know how you get down." She kissed my lips again and laid her head on my chest.

I looked around the small hotel room and tried my best to keep my composure. I knew what needed to be done. I had to out-think Rayjon and get my family and my crew out of his death-grip. Nobody other than me could do it. I had to master the game he was playin'.

Kenosha kissed my lips again. "Daddy, I already know you gotta go back out there tonight, but before you do, I need you to put me to sleep because my mind won't slow down. Can you please just do me real fast and hard like you always do and put yo' baby to sleep. Huh?" She started to unbuckle my belt, then opened my pants, sliding her hand inside of my boxers and pulling on my dick, squeezing it.

I closed my eyes as more tears fell down my face. It was all becoming so much to deal with at one time. I had so many people I had to provide for and make sure stayed straight. I felt like I was losing myself. I needed to be healed. I needed to take a break. I needed some form of an escape, but since there was no place I could be besides where I was, stuck in the position I was in, I decided to escape deep within the pits of Kenosha.

I don't know how it happened or when all my clothes came off, but the next thing I knew I had Kenosha lying on her left side with her leg over my right shoulder, and I was pounding her out like I was mad at her. I mean I was digging deep within her pussy and going as fast as I could with my teeth clenched. Her juices oozed out of her box as if she was peeing or somethin', and it motivated me to hit it even harder.

"Uh! Uh! Uh! Uh! Uh! Mm! Racine! Racine! Slow. Down. I. Daddy, I. Uh, shit! You fucking. Me. So. Hard!" She closed her eyes, grabbed the pillow, and bit into it, screaming deep within the pits of her throat.

I was in a far-away zone. While my dick went in and out of her pussy, I was trying to get my mind right. I had to find a way to master the game. I had so many enemies coming at my head. My back was against the wall, and my daughter's life was on the line. Her survival depended on me. Everything had to be conquered by me. It would be the only way for us all to prevail. I could not allow my shoulders to crumble. I had to make it happen for my baby girl first, and then Kenosha and my crew.

I flipped Kenosha over and pulled her up to her knees, pushed her face into the bed, grabbed her hips, and slid back into her pussy hard. "No! No! No! Daddy. Please. You. Fuckin'. The shit. Out of me. Please! Uh. Uh. Oh! Shit, daddy! Please. Mm. Shit!"

Her ass bounced back into my lap again and again. Her pussy was drooling all down my thighs. Our skins slapped together, and Kenosha kept on trying to reach out for somethin' to grab onto, but there was nothin' that could help her. I needed her body. I needed the warmth of her insides. Only her pussy could heal me. I had to release all my hurt and worries deep within her womb, as I always did, so I hit it as hard as I could while tears fell down my cheeks. Repeatedly, my mental struggles played before my eyes.

I fucked her all night until I came up with the solution to all my problems. While I was deep within her womb, I concocted the perfect plan of action.

After I came in Kenosha, I slowly pulled out and curled up alongside her, stroking her curly hair and kissing her on the back of the neck. "I love you, li'l momma. I hope you know that. I'll do anything for you, and I promise I'm finna go and get our daughter back." I kissed the back of her neck again, tasting the sweat. The saltiness, for some reason, made me love her even more. I was crazy about Kenosha and had always been.

She reached behind her and patted the side of my hip. "Daddy, I'm sorry for walking around the house like that while Tez was there, but you already know I would never cross you like that. I ain't ever gave no nigga the pussy since our daughter been born almost eight years ago. I know you do your thing out there and all, but that'll never make me get down like that. I love you way too much. I swear I do. Oh, and thank you for hitting this pussy the way it needed to be hit. That's another reason why I'd never step out on you." She yawned, then covered her mouth. "G'on out there and handle yo' bitness now, baby. I'm about to go to sleep while my body still tingling."

The more I lay in that bed looking down on her, the further I fell in love with my daughter's mother and knew I had to go out there and make it happen.

T.J. EDWARDS

Chapter 12

I met up wit' E and Tez less than an hour later. I was completely thrown off guard when Tez pulled up with three li'l niggaz in the back of his truck. I though I recognized them from the incident we had at the Taylors a few days ago.

"Look, Racine, these my li'l hitters. From now on I ain't rolling around without my security until I find out who trying to kill us at every turn. We got so many enemies out here in Chicago that it could be anybody. Fuck that. I'd rather one of these li'l niggaz get hit before I do, so until further notice, I'ma keep some shooters wit' me." He nodded his head at the three li'l niggaz still sitting in his truck a li'l distance away.

I felt what he was on. I just didn't think things through that thoroughly at the time. Since we were snatching up new turf and taking over a new ward, it was plenty li'l niggaz that was trying to be down wit' our mob. Most of them were send-offs and could be used as shields. What my cousin was doing had been done in Chicago since the beginning, starting wit' Al Capone.

"Bruh, long as you know what you doing, I'll never question you. I been fuckin' wit' you for a long time now, so let's just handle this bitness."

E tilted his bag of Doritos and put the opening to his mouth, allowing the rest of the chips to fall in there before he balled up the bag and threw it on the concrete. Then he wiped his hands off on a moist towelette, though I didn't know where he got it. "On some real shit, when it's my time to go, it's my time to go. I'm my own shooter. I don't put my life in nobody else's hands but my own. Say, Racine, when we go in this bitch, I got you. I'm riding for you until the dirt. I mean that shit." He took a .45 off his hip and cocked it back, replaced it, then did the same thing wit' a .9 millimeter. His face remained scrunched up the whole time.

I gave him a half hug. "I love you, nigga, and I already know what it is. Now, let's handle this bitness so you can get yo' ass back home to Nancy." Nancy was E's baby mother and probably the only female he cared about for real. I'd called him at, like, three thirty in the morning that night and he had been in bed, laid up with her. Once he told her he was leaving to come and fuck wit' me, she'd snapped out. They had been trying to get things in order amongst themselves for their son's sake.

"Bruh, don't worry about her. I got that. Let's handle this bitness, then body that nigga Rayjon like we should have did way back when."

I was ready to move and make shit happen. Once again Rayjon had not told me what I would be running into when I kicked in the door to the lick he gave me, so me and my crew was gon' have to go in there on straight bitness. He wanted everybody in the house dead, as usual, but at the same time he wanted us to come up with the merchandise that was inside. It was a rubix cube of a lick, difficult to say the least, but it had to be done. Had to be done because Madison's life was still at stake.

When it was all said and done, we found ourselves outside of an all-white, two-story mansion with a big metal gate that covered the entire property. From outside of the gate I could see six foreign cars in the driveway and two Hummers. I didn't know what to think other than whoever we were about to hit had to be caked up.

E crept to the side of me as I bent down by the gate. Crickets could he heard in the background, along with the water sprinklers that were going off as we overlooked the property. The only plus side to any of it was the fact the next property had to be about fifty acres away from the one we were crouching down in front of.

E shook his head that was covered by his ski mask. He cocked the side of his AK-47 assault rifle. "Bruh, wait a minute. I think I know whose shit this is. Fuck," he said and switching knees. I adjusted my eyeholes in my mask, so I could see more clearly.

"What you mean, fuck? What, it's the police or somethin'?" I asked, looking him over closely.

He shook his head. "Hell nall, that the nigga King's property. He run wit' them Young Radical niggaz that took over the Stateway Projects and injected all them old heads wit' that Virgin drug back in the day. He run wit' a nigga named Chris. They bullying the game wit' they heroin, and they got plenty killaz that's behind them. Bruh, these niggaz ain't the ones to be fuckin' wit' unless we ready to war wit' they ass wit' both barrels, trust me."

I knelt there for a second, looking over the mansion. I did remember hearing some shit about some niggaz taking over the Stateway Projects back in the day by kicking in doors and forcing the tenants to inject their powerful-ass heroin. Supposedly they'd repeated the same process with the Ada B. Wells Projects as well. The name King definitely rung throughout the slums.

Tez came over and crouched down on the side of me. "Cuz, you know this King shit, right? We can't go in there on no bullshit. We gotta go in there and let them hammers ride if this who Rayjon trying to have us hit. This nigga is Chicago, through and through. I'm finna go pop the trunk." He got up and jogged back to the Chevy Caprice he'd stolen for this hit.

I didn't know who exactly King was, but I was about to find out because his life was standing in the way of my daughter's. I didn't give a fuck about him or his Young Radicals. All I wanted was his life and the merchandise inside.

Tez came over and gave me an AR-15. "This what we gon' need for them. I'm ready, though, and so is my shooters."

The sun looked like it was on the verge of rising. I knew we had to make this happen under the cover of darkness because we were already in an uppity-type neighborhood. I didn't know how their police was out there, and I didn't want to find out.

Five minutes later I was lowering my AR-15 assault rifle over the fence and climbing over the top of the big metal fence while Tez and E did the same thing. As soon as my feet hit the grass, my heart started to beat fast as hell. I looked around and didn't locate any cameras or nothin' like that, but it didn't stop me from being super paranoid. I picked up my rifle and ran full speed toward the mansion, hunched over, ready to get on bitness. I wound up at the side patio door. The sun was starting to make more of an appearance, and I knew we had to get going.

I knelt down wit' Tez beside me and looked through the patio door's window. It appeared a big-screen smart television had been left on. There was a bowl of weed on the table. Next to that was a tin platter of what looked like cocaine from the distance I was peering from.

Tez shook his head. "These some major niggaz, cuz, but I'm wit' you. I ain't gon' lie and say I ain't worried, because I am, but nevertheless, it's me and you, ma nigga, until the world blow."

E came over, knelt down, then took his glasscutter and made a circle in the glass. He pushed it in slightly before stickin' his hand through it and unlocking the door. It clicked, then he started to pull it outward slowly. "Let's go, bruh. Catch these niggaz while they sleeping."

Once the door was open, he slipped inside. I followed him with my red beam activated on the top of my rifle. The mansion was dimly lit, but dark enough for my beam to illuminate across the room.

Tez sent his shooters in front of him, and they went in the opposite direction of me and E. We slowly made our way down the long hallway with

E out front and me covering his back. I was low to the ground, creeping like a Navy Seal. With each step my knees popped, and I clenched my teeth harder. The hallway was covered in white carpet that felt soft under my feet.

As we continued to make our way down the hall, I heard a shower running to my right. That caused me to stop and stand in front of that door. E paused, too, but I waved him off. "I got this bruh you hit up them other rooms," I whispered wit' my hand on the doorknob.

E nodded, then made his way further down the hall. I slowly twisted the door handle, then pushed it in. The further the door went in, the louder the shower water became, and then I got to hearing moaning.

"Uh. Uh. Uh. Yes. Yes. Yes. Uh. Oh, baby. Yes, Prince," came the female voice.

I opened the door all the way now with confidence. I knew that if there was a nigga in here fucking, he wouldn't have time to react the way he was supposed to, so I sped up my steps. I could see the silhouettes of three bodies all over each other.

I smiled and raised my rifle, getting ready to open the shower door, when *bam*! Something crashed into the back of my head and knocked me forward. I grew dizzy immediately and fell into the shower glass, shattering it.

"Ah! Ah!" came the screams from one of the females. Glass had shattered all over her. She slumped down in the stall, nearly sitting on me

SKI MASK CARTEL 3

while the male and the other female jumped out of the stall and tried to make a run for it.

It was then I looked up to see a big, muscular dude with a billy club in his hand. The water splashed into my face, and I could feel the blood running down the back of my neck and into my vest.

The man dropped the billy club to the floor and went to his waist and pulled out a .45, cocking it back. Written across his face was anger and disgust. "You bitch-ass nigga." He aimed his pistol as the naked threesome ran past him.

"Ah!" came the female's scream from the hallway.

"Bitch, move!" *Boom! Boom! Boom!* "Bitch-ass nigga, get the fuck off my homie!" E said, blowing the big dude's brains out the side of his head and against the wall. He slumped to the floor with his eyes wide open and a big hole in his head. Then E turned around and ran back into the hallway. I could hear the females screaming before the hallway lit up again and again.

Boom! Boom! Boom! Boom! "No!" *Boom! Boom!*

I got to my feet and stumbled for a few seconds, dizzy from the blow. I made my way into the hallway just as E was stepping back from one of the dead bodies with his handgun smoking. He looked over at me. "Come on, big homie. That nigga ran this way."

I followed him down the hall, then stepped over the two dead females in the middle of the carpet with their heads blown off. I felt some type of way because I felt like they were just at the wrong place at the wrong time, but I couldn't dwell on it. I stepped over them and followed E.

By the time we got into the big living room, Tez was throwing a nigga on his stomach and stomping him in the back. *Whoom!* "Bitch-ass nigga, shut the fuck up. Now, tell me where that dope at or I'm blowing yo' head off." Tez's shooters threw two other niggaz on to their stomachs and gave them the same treatment.

I followed E past the living room and down some stairs. Once we got there, he made a left. Stopping outside of a door, he took a step back before kicking it in, causing the door burst inward and hit the wall with force.

As soon as it flew in, the shots came. *Boom! Boom! Boom! Boom!*

E leaped in the air and flew backward before lying on his side.

Boom! Boom! Boom! I felt a slug punch me in the chest, knocking me off my feet and onto my ass. Luckily, I held onto my rifle and kept my eyes open. I saw it was two shooters who were preparing to run out of the room E had just kicked in, but not before I could aim that AR-15 and squeeze the trigger, letting that bitch ride. *Tat-tat-tat-tat-tat-tat-tat!* "Aw, you bitch-ass niggaz!" *Tat-tat-tat-tat-tat-tat!*

Fire spit from the barrel of my rifle, and the bullets ate into their flesh, choppin' them up from head to toe. The shooters stood in the room's doorway as hole after hole filled them. Finally, I stopped squeezing the trigger and they fell to the ground. I slid backward on my ass until I got to E, checking on my li'l homie. "E? E? Get up, nigga. Get up, bruh," I said, holding his head under my forearm.

Tez ran into the room with his assault rifle on his shoulder, looking all around. "What happened to the homie, cuz? Is he good?"

"Bitch-niggaz shot him. Them bitch-ass niggaz."

E jerked and opened his eyes, clenching his teeth together, blood dripped out of his mouth. "I'm good, bruh, just help me up. They got me, but I'm good."

As I stood up to help him to his feet, one of Tez's shooters came down the stairs with two .44 Desert Eagles. "What's good, chief? I heard shots, and –"

Boom! Boom! Boom! His head exploded before he fell backward against the steps, bleeding profusely.

Chick-chick. *Boom!* Chick-chick. *Boom!* Chick-chick. *Boom!* "Aw, shit!" Tez hollered and fell on his back.

I dropped to my knees and looked around for the shooter, but I couldn't see where the shots were coming from. I started to panic. I felt like I couldn't breathe, and my chest was killing me, blood constantly dripped down my neck.

Chick-chick. *Boom!* Chick-chick. *Boom!* A big chunk of wood flew off the wall and it was then I was able to discover which way the bullets were coming from. I looked to my left and saw a square opening in the floor, so I dropped to my belly and waited while Tez cried out in pain.

I low-crawled in the direction of the empty hole with my rifle against my shoulder I waited and got closer and closer. Then it happed, the shooter stuck his head up, along wit' his shotgun, and got ready to shoot in our direction again, but didn't count on me being ready for him. As soon as I saw that head pop up with the gun, I squeezed that trigger. *Tat-tat-tat-tat-tat!* The bullets crashed into his face, then his head disappeared back into the hole.

I got up and turned around to see Tez's shooter helping him up the stairs. I leaned down and picked up E. When we got back into the living room, I saw there were now six male bodies slain across the carpet. To the right of the couch was a big, black bag.

"Aw, shit. Cuz, grab that bag. It got all that shit in there Rayjon's bitch-ass wanted. Uh, fuck!" Tez groaned.

Crash! Tish! I looked up and saw a dude kicking in the glass of the patio door before running out into the night. He looked over his shoulder one time, fell, and got back up, continuing to run at full speed. I didn't know where he had been hiding at, but we had definitely slipped on him, and that would prove to be fatal soon.

We got back out to our whips wit' me and E in one and Tez and his last remaining shooter in another. "Tez, I gotta take you to the hospital," I hollered before we pulled off.

He shook his head at me, then I turned to E. "What about you? You need to go to the hospital?"

E winced in pain. "Nall, just drop me off at Nancy crib. She a nurse. She'll know how to handle this situation. I been here before."

With my chest killing me and hatred in my heart for Rayjon, I drove the homie right where he told me to, then made it back to the hotel with Kenosha.

While I was helping E onto Nancy's doorstep, he shook his head. "Nigga, you know we kilt King's son back there. We about to have drama like we never have before. We just gotta be ready."

I nodded my head, set him on the porch, and rang the doorbell, then Nancy came out and helped me take him into the house.

T.J. EDWARDS

Chapter 13

I wasn't asleep for more than two hours before Kenosha was waking me up by pushing me on the chest again and again. The pain was so horrible I woke up in tears.

"Stop. Stop. Stop. Baby, damn. I got shot right there last night," I said, pulling back the covers to show her how red my chest was. "You see this shit?"

She put both of her hands up to her face. "Oh my God, baby, I swear I didn't know. It's just that yo' phone been buzzing like crazy for the last hour off and on. I didn't want to answer it." She crawled across the bed and handed it to me, then kissed my chest softly.

I grabbed the phone and saw Wayne's number pop up. I texted him *'What's good?'* He texted back that he wanted to Facetime, so I made it happen.

He frowned into the screen. "Nigga, we got a problem." He sucked his gold teeth.

I tried to sit up in the bed better. I was sleepy, super tired, and my chest was killing me. "Uh. What's the problem, li'l homie?"

He frowned his face. "The problem is Denzell. That nigga is a rat and just ordered our hit. I can't let us go out like that." He took a step back and very quickly showed me his background. It appeared he had Denzell tied to a chair. Beside him was his wife, Janine. He brought his face back into the camera shot. "You see what I mean now, right? I need you to give me the head nod before I handle this bitness."

I shook my head, looking down at my phone. I didn't know what he was thinking to be recording that shit or Facetiming with them all tied up like that. That seemed real reckless to me. I looked closer at his eyes and saw they were bucked and glossy, which could have only meant he was on them fuckin' pills. Wayne had a habit of popping X, Oxy, and Percocet, which often clouded his judgment, so I didn't know if Denzell was actually ordering our hit or if the li'l homie was just tripping.

I ended the Facetime and told him to text me his location. Once he did that, I told him I would be there in a little while and to not do nothin' until I got there.

Kenosha leaned down and kissed my chest where I had gotten shot. I looked down at her lips as they came into contact with my skin. Even though her lips were real plump and juicy, every time they touched my injury it felt like a bee sting. I was thankful for the bulletproof vest, because had I not had it on, I would have probably been a dead man.

I winced from the pain and sat all the way up. "Baby, I gotta go handle some bitness. I don't want you leaving this room. Order from room service, anything you wanna eat, then lean back in the Jacuzzi for a li'l while."

I got up and started to get dressed, picking up my battered vest from the floor and putting it into place. "Ah, fuck!" I hollered out in pain immediately. The place where the bullet had slammed into the vest caused it to stick out a li'l bit, poking me. I adjusted it some and finished getting myself together.

Kenosha climbed out of the bed and kissed me on my back. "Daddy, please be careful out there. It seems like you getting hit up more and more lately. I don't know what I would do if something happened to you. I will not be in this world without you. I just can't." She wrapped her arms around me and laid her head on my back while I buckled my Gucci belt.

I turned around to face her, moving her curly hair out of her face and kissing her on the forehead. "I love you, Kenosha. I gotta just put out these last li'l fires, then we'll be able to move on with our lives, baby. It's just something I gotta do."

She looked up at me with her honey-brown eyes and blinked tears. "I get that, daddy, I really do, but I need you to be safe out there. I'm just letting you know that if anything happens to you, I'm not strong enough to move on with my life. Now, I don't know what that means entirely, and I don't want to find out. Just be safe and know I need you. We need you." She said this holding her stomach.

I nodded, then dropped to my knees and kissed her stomach before laying my face on her bare skin.

By the time I made it to Denzell's home where Wayne was keeping them hostage, Wayne had already cut off Denzell's ear and was threatening to do the same to his wife. I stepped into the den with my eyes opened wide.

"This fuck-nigga was gon' betray us, bruh. I got word from one of the people in his circle that he been fuckin' wit' them Stones out of Terror Town. They trying to move southward and take over the Taylors. They already gave this bitch-nigga a hunnit bands to make that move. Look." He stepped to his right, knelt down, and opened a briefcase full of hunnits. "You see this shit? Little did this bitch-ass nigga know, my cousin the prince of the Blackstones in that area. Prince Zakir run all that shit, and he got word to me immediately. All he want is his money back and this nigga's life, because this ain't the first time he had his hand in some shady shit like this. He got five of the Stones kilt last summer, and twenty of them indicted. His bitch-ass ain't right." Wayne walked over to him and slapped him so hard he and his chair fell sideways with blood running out of his ear socket.

Denzell was a city alderman that me and my crew made a deal with to take over the Taylors since it was in his ward. We were supposed to pay him a fee every week and drive the crime rate up in the next ward, which was ran by Julian Lewis. But after me and my crew took Julian's life, everything was supposed to be considered even. The Taylors should have been ours outright.

What Wayne was describing was something that took place in Chicago every single day. Double-dealing. Denzell was trying to sell one territory to different mobs in the hopes that one of us would kill the other off and he'd never be found out. That was some dirty shit, but it was life in Chicago at its darkest level.

Wayne picked his chair back up and punched him square in the mouth with all his might, I guessed, because one hit broke Denzell's nose and had it turnt awkwardly. "When I take this tape off, tell my nigga what the fuck you did or I'm stanking you right here and right now." He ripped the tape off and stood back with a mug on his face.

"Uh! Racine. Racine, I swear, man, I don't know what he's talking about. I – I."

Bam. Bam. Bam. Bam. Bam. "Muthafucka, you gon' lie?" *Bam. Bam. Bam.* One blow after the next. Wayne went on a rampage, whooping Denzell's ass. I mean he was hitting him so fast that by the time I got over to him to pull him back, there was blood all over the walls behind Denzell's chair.

I pulled Wayne back, and Denzell stayed hunched over with blood running from his nose and mouth. It dripped down like a red string of cheese. He coughed and spit a loogie on the wood floor.

"Okay. Okay. Fuck, just don't hit me no more." He spit again, then looked up with both of his eyes swollen. "I did it. I sold the land in my ward to you, Racine, and the Blackstones. But that's the way the game goes. Just like I'd previously sold it to J-Rock and you at the same time. You rose up and conquered him, knocked him off, making it your home. I never told the Stones they wouldn't have a war on their hands. I told them who was already in place over here just like I told you when you purchased my influence." He spit another bloody loogie. "Just tell me what I can do to save my life. Tell me what you need from me and I'll do it. I don't want to die, man. Please, it was just business."

Wayne stepped to the side of me and got ready to rush Denzell with the long knife in his hand, but I caught him, jumping in front of him with my arms out. "Man, li'l homie, chill."

He scrunched his face. "Chill? Man, fuck chilling. That bitch-ass nigga ain't got no loyalty in him. We bodied a whole fucking house for him, and this the thanks we get? Hell nall, nigga. I'm killing him and this bitch right here. Move, Racine."

He attempted to go around me, but I blocked his path.

"Racine, I'll put you in, man. I'll put you in with Capone. He'll get you rich. All this dope selling you doing in the hood ain't shit. You can do a whole lot better. He looking to make a deal wit' a vicious black crew like yours. Just give me a chance, man. Look, his number is right in my phone over there on the table. If you get it, we can call him and talk to him together. You'll be all the way in. I promise."

"Man, yo' promises don't mean shit to this cartel because you ain't got no loyalty, nigga! Let me kill this muthafucka, Racine. I'm begging you, ma nigga." His chest heaved up and down, and I could tell he was heated.

I shook my head. "Nall, not yet." I walked over, picked up his phone, and brought it over to where he sat tied up in the chair with blood all over his face. To the right of him Janine sat calmly with her eyes closed, as if she had been in that position a million times before.

"I can't believe you finna fuck wit' this snake-ass nigga, Racine! What the fuck is you thinking?" Wayne hollered, losing his cool.

I held up my hand. "Just chill, bruh. I got this shit." I started to scroll down his call log. "What's his name under?" I knew Don Capone had a lot of pull throughout the Midwest. He had his hands in all types of narcotics, guns, sex trafficking, I mean he did it all. If by some chance I could get my crew linked in with him for just a year, we could be millionaires before it was all said and done.

"It's under Resources. He'll pick up on the ninth ring," Denzell said, sounding out of breath.

I called the number and waited until the ninth ring. Sure enough, the mob boss answered just like Denzell said he would.

"Yello, what do you want on your pizza?"

I put the phone to Denzell's mouth, but not so close blood could get on the phone. I wasn't wit' that shit.

"Don, it's me, and I've got what you requested."

"Yeah, but a name is all you need at times," said Capone in a heavy Sicilian accent.

"The name's Racine. Smart kid. All the qualifications you need to run a restaurant out here in these parts. I'll have him send in an

161

application if you're still hiring," Denzell said, trying to sound as if everything was okay.

Capone was quiet for a long time. "I'm trusting your judgment. Have the kid bring the application directly to me, and if he is what you say he is, I'll hire him on the spot. *Capisce*?"

"Understood," Denzell returned, and then the phone hung up on the other end.

I memorized the number and dropped the phone at Denzell's feet. "Where would I go to meet somebody like him?"

Denzell tried to sit up in his seat, but I guessed his ribs were broken because as soon as he sat up straight he cried out in pain. "Ah! Fuck!" Then he started to breathe real heavy. "He has a meat-packing company off Jarvis on the north side. A place called Fiorino's. I always meet him there on Sundays between ten and eleven in the morning."

I nodded my head. "You a dirty nigga, Denzell. You don't give a fuck about yo' ward or the people inside of it. All you care about is money and yourself," I said, looking at him, disgusted.

Wayne stepped forward "That's why I gotta kill them. Fuck it, I'll start wit' the bitch if that make you feel better." He stepped in front of Janine and pulled the tape from her mouth. "You got anything you wanna say before I slice yo' throat?"

Tears fell from her cheeks. "Racine, please don't let him kill me. I have been nothing but good to you ever since you were a little boy. Now, you know I don't have nothin' to do wit' my

162

husband's indiscretions. He's an evil man, and I left him emotionally a long time ago," she sniffled.

Denzell spit out another bloody loogie. "Bitch, all you care about is my money. If they kill you, it'll be doing me a favor. That way you can't get half of my shit that you didn't work for. In fact, I'll tell you what, Racine. You let me go and kill her, I'll give you five hundred thousand dollars right now." He sat up and exhaled loudly, wincing in pain. "What'll you say?"

Janine looked me in the eye as tears ran down her cheeks. "He's evil, Racine, but I know you're not. Honey, if it's all about the money, there is a safe in our pool house."

"Shut up, bitch! Shut up! Kill that whore, Racine! Please!" Denzell hollered at the top of his lungs.

"Man, shut the fuck up!" I swung and punched him straight in the mouth as hard as I could, knocking him clean out. "Bitch-ass nigga!" He slumped over with his head in his lap.

I knelt in front of Janine, rubbing her cheek with my finger. "Tell me what you were going to say, Ms. Robinson." I resorted back to the name I was used to calling her when she was my teacher in elementary.

Tears dripped off her chin. "Baby, there is a safe in the pool house that has nearly four million dollars in cash. Along with that, it has paperwork of all the dirt he has on other senators and judges in this city. The combination is nine four times. You can have it all, just let me live," she pleaded.

I took a deep breath. "Where is the safe located?" I wiped away a few of her tears and looked her in her deep brown eyes.

"It's behind the picture of Barack Obama, right next to the fireplace.

"Li'l homie, go grab that. Take one of them garbage bags wit' you out of the kitchen, and hurry back." I said this looking Janine in the eye the whole time.

Wayne nodded at me, ran into the kitchen, then came out of it carrying a black garbage bag. "She betta not be lying, bruh, cuz if she is." He sucked his teeth, then ran out of the back door of the house.

As soon as he was outside, Janine started to cry harder. "I need you, Racine. I need you to save me, because your friend is going to kill me. I just know he is," she whimpered. "I don't deserve this, and you know it, baby. I've done all I could to ride beside that man but look where it's got me. This isn't fair in the least bit." Snot dripped out of her nose and onto her top lip.

"Ms. Robinson, I'm not gon' let nothin' happen to you. I promise. I know you ain't got shit to do wit' this. I can't let his sins fall on yo' shoulders. I'm better than that." I wiped her tears away, reached, grabbed a Kleenex, and wiped her nose for her. "You gon' be okay, you hear me?"

She swallowed and shook her head. "The life insurance policy on him is five million, Racine. Five million. You make this look like a robbery, kill him, injure me, and I'll give you half. I swear on my life."

Denzell stirred and sat up, wincing in pain once again. "I knew you wasn't shit, bitch. I knew you was a gold-digging bitch. I should've left yo' country-ass down in Missouri with the rest of yo' loser-ass family," he spat.

"Please, Racine, save me from him. Save me from his lifestyle. You can have it all. I won't say anything. I swear it."

Wayne came back into the Den carrying the big, black bag over his shoulder as if he was Santa Clause. "That bitch wasn't lying, bruh. It look like it's all here. Now, let's waste them and get the fuck out of here." He sat the bag down and pulled out the knife, walking toward Denzell.

I stood up. "Murk his ass, bruh. Make him pay for his disloyalty."

That was all Wayne needed to hear. He stepped forward and grabbed Denzell by the forehead, pushing it backward and exposing his throat, lifting the knife way over his head. "I never liked yo' punk-ass, nigga. You sell yo' people just like a slave master. Now rest in peace, fuck-nigga." He brought the knife down at full speed.

"Argh! Argh! Argh! Argh! Argh! Argh! Uh!" Denzell hollered as Wayne slashed him again and again across his throat. His arm started to move so fast it became a blur while Denzell's blood popped into the air.

Janine's eyes were opened wide, watching Wayne kill her husband. Then he stepped in front of her. "Bitch, you next."

She closed her eyes real tight. "Our Father, who art in Heaven, hallowed be thy name. Thy kingdom come, may thy will be done on Earth as it is done in Heaven. Give us –"

I tapped Wayne on the shoulder. "Nall, she good, bruh. I'm gon' handle this. You meet me outside."

He looked me over for a long time with his face scrunched up, then shrugged his shoulders. "A'ight, bruh, handle yo' bitness."

As soon as he disappeared, I knelt in front of Janine again. "Look, Ms. Robinson, you don't owe me nothing else. You take that money and you live good. I know you been through a lot. It's time you enjoy life in freedom."

She shook her head. "No, Racine. Let me take care of you. I owe you, baby, please. Let me give you half of the money."

I leaned forward and kissed her on the lips for a long time, then stood up. "You good. Live happy." I pushed her chair over and broke the right leg on it, then kicked his phone closer to her. That way it looked like she'd been rocking back and forth in her chair until the leg broke, and once it fell over, she was able to make her escape. Quite honestly, I didn't know how she was going to get out of that jam, but I felt confident she wouldn't spill the beans.

Chapter 14

That night Denzell's murder was all over the news. They labeled it as a home invasion, armed robbery, murder. The streets were hot as a firecracker, and the city of Chicago was demanding justice for their beloved, crooked alderman.

I really didn't have time to dwell on that because at five in the morning the next day Averie hit me up, and we met up in a Walmart parking lot. I got out of my truck and jumped into her pink Benz and greeted her with a kiss. "Hey, baby," I said, tasting her cherry lip gloss.

She smiled. "It's some family down here from out east that's on Rayjon's heels. It shouldn't be long until they close in and finish him off. Time is of the essence, and you need to get yo' daughter back or when they catch him, they gon' kill her, too."

I frowned and almost smacked the shit out of her. It would have been my first time putting my hands on a woman, and I felt like she would have deserved that lick. "What you mean, if they catch him first they might kill my daughter along with him? That mean I'm in a worse position now than I was in before you tried to help me."

The sky turned darker and there were a few raindrops coming across the windshield. Out the window, a lady with three kids ran while pushing her cart while her five-year-old daughter tried to keep up.

Averie shook her head. "Nall, I got the head you need in that duffle bag back there. I also got the two mill he saying he want. All you gotta do is either give him yo' cousin head for real or find one that looks close enough. The one I got of me, this bitch look like my twin. I had her face burned a bit for effect, but it should help you out just fine. All you gotta do is call him and set up a meeting and hurry up. I know how Aiden an' them work." She turned on her ignition just as the rain started to pour.

I reached into the backseat and grabbed the duffel bag. It felt real heavy. I couldn't help but think about Madison. By the way Averie was talking, I was beginning to think I would never see her again. I didn't know who Aiden was, but I felt she was trying to tell me I didn't have much time before I could save my daughter. I had to reach out to Rayjon right away. I didn't know what I would do if anything serious happened to my little girl. I felt myself ready to break down at the thought of it. "Look, Averie, I don't know what kind of pull you got wit' these niggaz but tell them to give me one more day. I'll be out of their way, and they can have Rayjon. Don't let them hurt my daughter, Averie, please."

She turned to look at me, then shook her head before putting her hand on my thigh. "I lost my son to this game, Racine, so it's making it real hard for me to sympathize wit' you right now because I already know how this shit goes. However, I really do love you, and I will do all I can to delay them, but I'm telling you I mean nothin' to them in the grand scheme of things. They just didn't know what city he'd escaped to. I told them and kept my life, now I have to disappear again. Things are real crazy, but you'll soon find out. I wish I could do more for you, but right now I just –"

Boom!

The window shattered, and Averie's brains splashed all over my face and neck before her car door was yanked open, followed by mine. As soon as mine opened, the barrel of a Mossberg pump was put to my forehead by Rayjon. "Get yo' stupid ass out the car and into the back of that truck over there. Hurry up, and don't make no scene." He said this looking over his shoulder as the rain picked up and splashed off the brim of his fitted New York Yankees cap.

I looked and saw an all-black Navigator parked in the middle of the parking lot with the back door opened. People were scrambling all around us to make it to their cars after hearing the loud gunshot that could not be masked by the thunder that roared overhead.

Once in the back of the Navigator, I looked out the window to see Rayjon snatch the duffle bag out of the car, then jog over and jump into the passenger's seat. Inside the truck were two-armed men I had not paid much attention to because I was still in shock from seeing Averie's head get blown off. I felt sick to my stomach.

Rayjon slammed the door to the truck and laughed. "What type of bitch cross a nigga and then do bitness in the same whip he bought her ass?" He shook his head. "A dumb bitch, that's what type. Racine, you a dumb-ass nigga. You chose to fuck wit' that bitch over me, and now look at her. Hmm." He shook his head again and laughed. "I guess that's my money in this bag, huh? You had Averie's ass working like a muthafucka." He nodded. "I like that in you."

Averie's blood dripped down my forehead and onto my cheeks. It felt like oatmeal. I knew it was mostly her brain matter. "Look, Rayjon, that's two million dollars right there, homie. Our debt should be cleared." I sat up and looked out the window, trying to determine where he was taking me.

He turned around to look at me. "Oh, nigga, you think it's gon' be that easy? After all the shit you and that bitch took me through?" He shook his head. "Nall, nigga. Besides, I still need yo' cousin head. That nigga crossed me, too. And this money I got on my own, which mean you still owe me two million. So, what the fuck is you talking about, li'l nigga?" He mugged me and lowered his eyes.

I looked him in the eyes with hatred. I was tired of this nigga, tired of playin' by his rules. I missed my daughter, and I wanted her home, so I could get her and Kenisha out of Chicago and some place safe. But for any of those things to happen, I had to get rid of Rayjon after I got my daughter back.

"Let's take this bitch-nigga to the sewer and teach him a lesson. I wanna break some shit on him so he can understand this shit ain't a game.

Head toward the Pier," Rayjon said, and I saw the big driver nod his head and grunt. "You hear that, Racine? I'm finna take yo' ass down to this sewer and break some of yo' bones. After I'm done, I might let you see yo' daughter. She losing a whole lot of weight now cuz she won't eat shit, but that's just how the cookie crumbles, huh?"

I felt my temper go red hot. I couldn't take no more. I imagined Madison down in those sewers in one of the rooms he'd created, and it made me hot. My vision got blurry, and I knew I was about to lose control. There was a heavyset dude sitting next to me with his gun laying lazily at his side. I sized him up from the corner of my eye.

The driver turned onto the highway before increasing his speed.

"Yeah, Racine, every time I tried to feed the li'l bitch, she acted like she was sick or somethin', so I just let her starve. Kinda like you and Averie hoped I was gon' do when you betrayed me wit' that bitch! You crossed a savage nigga. I hope yo' punk ass daughter dead by the time we get there!" He snapped before turning around in his seat.

I was boiling. I got to looking at the back of that nigga's head as he sat in the seat in front of me, imagining Madison all alone and afraid. Then I thought about how Rayjon had just killed a female he had been with ever since they were kids. He killed her with no mercy or regard. I knew if he could kill her like that, neither me nor Madison stood a chance.

He laughed and tilted his chair back. "I kilt that bitch, kid. Best feeling I done felt in a long time, too. You next, Racine."

My heart got to beating so fast I could barely breathe. I took my elbow and slammed it into the dude's temple who sat next to me and grabbed the gun off his lap, cocking it. *Boom!* His noodles flew out of the window along with the bullet that shattered the glass.

Rayjon tried to let his seat up, but I was already in the front of the truck with him and the driver. I put the pistol to his head and pressed it hard against his temple. "Fuck-nigga, don't move or I swear I'ma kill you."

He smacked the gun away from his face and reached on his waist. "Kill me then, nigga. This shit ain't sweet!" He went to aim his gun at me and pulled the trigger. *Boo-wah! Boo-wah!*

I jumped to the side just in time. His bullet slammed into the driver's face. The driver's head hit the steering wheel, causing the horn to blare loudly. *Beep!*

Boo-wah! Boo-wah! Two bullets slammed into the roof of the truck while the truck started to veer off course, crashing into the side of a purple Neon. Still we tussled for his gun. It was difficult for me because I still had my own gun in my hand, trying to find a window to put one in his head, but he was stronger than I thought.

He tackled me against the dead driver. The dead dude's foot became lead on the gas pedal. The truck sped up and crashed into the divider while me and Rayjon wrestled for the guns.

"Bitch-ass nigga, you gon' die. Then I'ma kill yo' daughter. I'ma cut that li'l bitch up Jersey-style, ma nigga."

He tried to stick his gun in my face, and by the way I was holding my own pistol, it bent my finger backward awkwardly, causing me to drop my gun and fight him for his. "Uh! Uh! Fuck-nigga. Preying on kids? What part of the game is that?"

I tried to sling him off me when he kneed me in the nuts. All the air left me immediately, and I threw up right on my chest.

Rayjon straddled me all the way with a smile on his face, the gun now fully in his possession. "Yeah, kid. Lights out time. Night-nights." He cheesed his teeth.

Err! Crash! The truck jerked us both forward so hard we flew into the windshield at the same time, then it started to roll. My head hit the ceiling, then the door, then the steering wheel. Then the driver's dead body landed on top of me, and I could feel the blood running into my eyes. I grew dizzy and couldn't locate Rayjon.

Err! Crash! Err! Bam! The truck jerked from side to side as one car crashed into it after the next. I felt like a pinball inside of a pinball machine. Blood continued to drip into my eyes. I could hear sirens off in the distance.

I pushed the dead body off me, looked over, and saw Rayjon lying on his back with a big gash on the side of his head, bleed profusely. He opened the passenger's door and jumped out, making his way across the highway that stood still because of the huge crash.

The sirens got louder and louder. Somehow, some way, I willed myself to climb out of the driver's side window. I fell to the pavement on my stomach and rolled to my side, then forced myself to stand up. A deep pain shot up from my groin where Rayjon had kneed me. I could barely breathe, but as I looked down the highway I could see the lights of three police cars. I knew I couldn't stay there and allow myself to get caught. I took a deep breath and breathed it out very slowly.

Twenty yards away from me Rayjon made his way across the highway and up the hill of grass on the side of. The hill led back to Cottage Grove Street. I wanted to chase him down. I needed to put an end to all his madness and make it to the sewers and get Madison before he could.

People started to get out of their cars all around me. I looked at the truck we'd been driving in and saw the dude I'd shot hung halfway out of the back passenger's window with blood coming from the hole in his head.

I shook my head and snapped out of it. There was no way I was going to catch Rayjon now. He was too far away and creating a further distance in between us. To my left I saw the El train coming down its tracks about a hunnit yards down. I had to make it to the platform before it came, it would be my only chance of getting out of the area as the sirens of the cop cars got closer.

174

I ran as fast as my body would allow me, got to the concrete divider that separated the train from the cars that drove along the highway, and jumped over it, landing on the tracks. The train couldn't have been more than fifty yards away.

A sharp pain shot from my groin again, this time causing me to hunch over and holler, "Aw! Shit!" I felt like I wanted to break down on my knees and cry because the pain was so intense, but I had to will myself forward, which is what I did. With all the fight left in me, I ran across the tracks and jumped to get ahold of the bottom of the platform, pulling myself up.

As soon as I got to the top of the platform, the Howard and Dan Ryan train pulled up, screeching on its tracks. There were only two other people waiting for the train, and I was hoping neither one of them pulled out a cell phone. If they had, I would've had to cause them bodily harm. There was two dead bodies left in that truck, and I was sure to have gunpowder residue on my hands, so at the very least I was going down for one of the murders.

Luckily for me, nobody pulled out a phone, and when the train pulled in I got on and sat where I could see both patrons who had witnessed the crash. As the train was pulling away, the cops were struggling to make their way through the car pile-up. I noted a bunch of people were pointing at the train and in the direction, Rayjon had disappeared.

I already knew I wasn't going to stay on the El long, and I didn't. I rode it for two stops and then got off. Fifteen minutes later Wayne was pulling up and I was jumping into his whip on 55th and Garfield.

"We gotta get to the sewers right now, bruh. That's where that nigga keeping my daughter at," I said, trying to breathe slowly. My nuts were killing me, and I felt like I wanted to throw up.

"The sewers? What do you mean? How do you know he keeping her down there?" he asked, pulling off into traffic and then getting onto the highway.

"That fool just smoked Averie, then he was getting ready to do me in. He thought he had me where he wanted me, so he exposed his hand, bruh. I know for a fact that's where he keeping my baby. You gotta head north. You know the entrance to them right by the Navy Pier?"

Wayne nodded, then stepped on the gas. "Man, I'm so tired of this nigga, cuz. Name any other nigga we would have let live this long after crossing somebody in our cartel? You can't, ma nigga, because we'd never let that shit happen. I'm ready to knock this punk's head off." He frowned, reached into his inside pocket, and popped two pills, swallowing them without water.

I didn't know what he just took, but I hoped it didn't throw him off his game when it came down to us handling bitness to get Madison back. "Look, bruh, that nigga was on foot, but I'm pretty sure that's where he headed. I feel like if we make it there before he do, then we got a good chance of getting her back and bringing her home, safe and sound. All I want is my baby back, Wayne.

Then we can kill everything that got that fool's last name. I ain't playin', either."

I kept thinking about Madison tied up in the sewers, starving or sick or something. We had hit a few licks wit' Rayjon where we'd left a victim tied up wit' no food for two days until they told us everything we needed to know, and by everything, I mean combinations to safes and locations. I hated imagining my baby being on that end of things. It made me feel like a straight sucka.

Wayne shook his head. "This nigga playin' wit' our kids, Racine. What type of shit is that, bruh? You already know I ain't playin' about mine, I would have made that nigga put up or lay the fuck down. I'm kamikaze. I can't help that." He sucked his teeth. "I ain't kill Toya, either, man. I was gonna, but then I thought about it. Ever since I known her she been one hunnit wit' me. This ain't the first lick I done hit that she put together, and I ain't never had to worry about her running her mouth. I don't know if that baby mine or not, but I'ma see. She did say Tim raped her a few times, him and that nigga Casey, but she saying that was months back, and besides that she ain't fucked nobody but me. The times add up, so I'ma do right by her until I find out otherwise." He nodded. "I guess I'm telling you this because she seen all of our faces, and I know her being alive falls on my shoulders. I just wanna let you know I would never jeopardize our crew, and I'm on top of all of this. If I detect anything shady from her end, I'm bodying her, bruh. You got my word on that." He looked over to me and smiled weakly.

"Li'l homie, that was yo' mission. You ran point. I trust you, and I know you gon' be on top of shit. I'm glad you thought about it before you just kilt her. You'd never forgive yourself if you had, especially if there is a chance that baby she carrying is yours." Just mentioning the word baby made me think about Madison. My throat got tight, and I was doing everything I could to keep my composure.

When we pulled up to the entrance of the sewers where Waste Management of Chicago were usually staked out, I damn near passed out at what I saw. I mean my heart started to beat so fast I really couldn't breathe.

Wayne looked at me with his eyes bucked. "Fuck, Racine. Bruh, don't panic. This don't necessarily mean what you thinking." He looked back out the window and shook his head.

Chapter 15

Everywhere I looked there was a police car with sirens blaring. If it wasn't a police car, there was a fire truck or ambulance. I started to imagine the worst. I didn't know how I was going to take it if I found out Madison was found dead. I didn't think I was strong enough to handle that. I swallowed, not knowing what to do as the sun set behind the clouds.

I was just getting ready to open my door when Wayne grabbed my arm. "Bruh, that'd be stupid as hell. It's police everywhere out there. They gon' snatch yo' ass up, and you ain't never gon' see the light of day again. It ain't nothing you can really do for her right now. If she in there, then it's a one-hunnit percent guarantee the police got her. And if it's the worst-case scenario, God forbid, then we gon' find out about it anyway on the news. You go out there asking questions wit' all of the shit we done did hanging over our heads, man, you asking for trouble." He said this while looking out the window at the scene.

There were police officers running back and forth, then into the tunnel of the sewers, followed by firemen. The ambulance had the back doors open as if it were waiting on a body to be brought inside of it, and there was a sea of people gathering around, trying to see what was going on.

"We gotta go, Racine. You know we do. What do you say, man?" he asked, looking me over closely.

I blinked, and tears fell down my cheeks. I just felt like something wasn't right. I felt like I had lost my daughter without it actually being confirmed. I felt myself becoming undone. I missed her so much, and I wanted to run out of that car, rush into that sewer and find her, but I knew that would have been the dumbest thing for me to do. Everything Wayne said made sense, and as much as I hated to admit it, he was right. I had to follow my common sense and not my emotions. "Let's go, bruh, before I get outta this muthafucka and run in there looking for my baby."

He nodded his head. "Look, man, I love you, Racine. And trust me, I'm wit' you. We in this shit together, one way or the other. Ski Mask for life, ma nigga. Loyalty over everythang."

We didn't say a word to each other as he drove away from the scene and back into the city. We just listened to the Adrenalin Rush CD by Twista and collected our thoughts. Mine were on Madison. I don't know why, but I kept on imaging her lying in a casket. I know that don't sound right, being as I was her father, but it was just somethin' in me that always made me assume the worst about everything. I felt like I had done so much wrong in the world that my sins were destined to come back to haunt me or take away the ones I loved the most. I felt sick.

I hated myself for losing Madison. I needed her and wished I could see her beautiful face one more time. I wished I could kiss her soft cheeks. She was my everything. It took all the strength in the world for me to not break down right there in Wayne's passenger seat.

Wayne's phone buzzed as he pulled up to a red light. He read the text, then started to shake his head like crazy. "No. No. No. Fuck no." He slammed on the gas and shot through the red light, then made a U-turn and almost hit a white dude crossing the street before flooring his Benz, taking it to top speeds.

I sat up in my seat and looked both ways, trying to see if any police were around. "Bruh, what's good?" I asked, looking him over very closely.

He started mumbling to his self. "The Stones just shot up my baby mother crib wit' my daughter in there." He swallowed. "They already kilt my cousin."

He said the last part so low I could barely hear him. I sat back in my seat and exhaled loudly. "Fuck, it's like this shit never ends. Well, since I'm waiting to see what take place wit' my li'l girl, let's go and handle yo' bitness. I'm wit' you one-hunnit percent, but you can't be speeding downtown like this or we ain't gon' make it back to the city." I said this looking around for the law. I didn't spot any of them. They were probably held up at the sewers, which at this moment was a good thing.

Wayne turned a corner hard, then sped up before jumping back onto the highway. "I already know who did this shit, bruh. It's my cousin's right-hand man, because when he found out my cousin bowed down and let us keep the Taylors

T.J. EDWARDS

without bringing no heat our way, he felt some type of way about it. That nigga don't like me because I used to bang with them Folk niggaz. You know they still at war wit' them? And since I used to be on the frontlines knocking they heads off, he holding a grudge against me. But I got this nigga. I'm finna tear some shit up over mines, believe that." As he drove, he started to text on his phone.

I didn't know who he was getting at or what he was saying, but I knew it was about to go down. That was Chicago, there was always one war inside of another one. The more niggaz a person fucked wit', the more wars they became a part of. To be loyal meant something totally different here.

Wayne stayed on 71st and Bishop, so as we came to the street I thought he was about to turn down it, but instead he drove two blocks over and pulled up in front of a green duplex. As soon as he did, I looked up toward the house and saw his daughter open the door and run down the stairs at full speed. He opened his driver's side door and met her in front of the car. She ran right into his arms, and he picked her up.

I got out and looked around. There were people everywhere out there. They looked onto the scene, nosey as Wendy Williams. I didn't have a pistol on me, and I felt like I needed one. I felt naked without it. I knew for a fact I had hit-up a few of the niggaz that ran in this hood. They were Gangsta Disciples, and for a long time me and Tez

182

used to haunt them because they were making so much money in the Englewood area.

"Daddy, I almost got shot. They put a whole bunch of bullets in my momma's house," Wayneisha whimpered before breaking into tears against the homie's shoulder. She wrapped her arms around his neck and her legs around his waist.

Wayne hugged her with his eyes closed, then opened them and looked at me with a mug on his face. "It's okay, baby girl. I got you now. Daddy ain't gon' let nothing happen to his baby. You hear me, Princess."

She nodded her head. "They kilt Zakir, too. They shot him up and left him in the middle of the street. I'm so scared, Daddy. What if they come looking for me?" she cried and really broke into sobs.

Wayne bounced her up and down, trying to console her. I could see his face, and it was that of anger. I had never seen him look so mad for as long as I knew him. I understood we was gon' be handling bitness ASAP. I would have wanted to do the same thing. The worst part of the game was allowing something to happen to the ones I loved, or when something happened to them I couldn't control. A father never wanted to see his baby girl shed tears or know she'd been under attack and he'd not been there to save her.

Wayne started to carry her up the stairs. "Look, Racine, I'm finna go in here and make sure my baby straight. I'll be back out in a minute, then we gon' go and get these niggaz, right? I don't play about my seed, man. This my heart, right here. I can't accept this." He carried her up the stairs and disappeared into the downstairs residence.

I pulled out my phone and looked it over. I had ten missed calls, five from Kenosha and five from Ellie. I was about to go over the messages when something told me to look up and across the street. When I did, I noted a group of about fifteen niggaz had formed, rocking blue and black with their hats turned to the right. I knew from experience I was in Gangsta Disciple territory. Them niggaz were savages, and they didn't play with the opposition. I felt my heart pounding in my chest right away.

Slowly, I made my way to the car when some li'l young nigga who couldn't have been older than twelve stepped from the crown of niggaz with a Mach .11 in his hands.

"Say, fool, what you doing around here? You know this Folks hood, right?" He walked across the street for a few paces, then raised the Mach and aimed it at me. "Put yo' hands up, my nigga." At saying this, he pulled a blue bandana over his face.

I lowered my head, then looked over to him. "Look, bruh, I ain't on shit. I know where I'm at. I ain't got no problem wit' Folks. My li'l homie's people just got shot up, and I'm over here wit' him making sure they straight."

The li'l boy walked closer to me and stopped at about four feet in front of me, looking back over his shoulder at the crew of savages behind him as if looking for permission to splash me. "Say the

184

word, big Folk, and I'll kill this nigga right here and right now. That's on the GI."

People started to slip into their houses, grabbing their kids by the arm and disappearing as fast as they could. I was fuming. I hated being in that position. I felt helpless and like once again my life was on the line for that day.

The wound on my forehead started to bleed again. It dripped down into my eye, and I didn't even wipe it away.

"What you say, big Folk? Should I kill this nigga or not?" he hollered, looking me in the eye.

Just then Wayne came out of the house, saw what was going on, and threw his hands in the air. "Aye! Hold on, that my nigga right there. He ain't the enemy." He ran over to where the li'l nigga had me at gunpoint, snatched the gun away from him, and smacked him so hard he fell to the ground, holding his mouth. "You li'l bitch-ass nigga. Didn't I just say this my dude right here?" He yanked him up and put the Mach to his cheek. "How you like it, huh? Bitch-ass nigga? That's my muthafucking nigga! He ain't the enemy," he said through clenched teeth.

"A'ight! A'ight! I didn't know. I swear I didn't," the li'l boy whimpered while the crowd of niggaz across the street looked on and laughed. I made it my bitness to remember some of their faces. I was gon' make sure I hit some of they ass up over this shit. There was no way somebody wasn't gon' pay for the sins of that li'l boy.

Wayne took the clip out of the Mach and handed both the gun and the clip to the li'l boy.

"Get yo' li'l ass out of here, Travis, and quit letting them niggaz send you off," he ordered, muggin' the group across the street.

We jumped in his whip with my temper blazing. I wanted to snap the fuck out, but I knew now wasn't the time. I had to let Wayne get out his frustrations on the kats that shot up his daughter's mother's crib. "So, what's the move, bruh?" I asked, trying to calm down.

"I finna switch this whip, hop in the van, then scoop E and Tez. Them niggaz, along wit' a few shooters, gon' ride out wit' us to hit up these Stone niggaz. They got this li'l temple they go to over here on Colfax. We should be able to hit, like, twenty of they ass and make a statement. I'm moving my daughter out of this city, too," he said.

I was down to ride out wit' him and get it over wit'. My mind was on Madison. I was hoping I didn't discover any bad news pertaining to her, which is why I neglected to look over Kenosha's messages. I just wasn't ready to receive that kind of news. "A'ight, let's do this, then."

I wanted to get this mission over, so I could finally have the space to focus on my situation. Deep down in the pits of my mind I was praying my daughter wasn't found in that sewer. It was literally taking all the strength I had inside of me to not breakdown over imagining the worst.

After switching whips and loading up in the van, we pulled up to Nancy's house just as E was coming out of it with a long trench coat on. He had his right arm tucked inside of the coat, and as he was coming down the stairs he looked both ways as if he were paranoid. I also noted a faint limp.

I slid open the side door and he jumped in with a mug on his face. "Wayne, we should've got at these niggaz a long time ago. I already knew that shit with the Taylors wasn't just gon' blow over like that. It's plenty mobs out here that want them buildings. It's only right the Stones would come for it since they ain't that far away and all they fuck wit' is heroin. The Robert Taylor Home Projects is the most heroin-infested area in the city of Chicago. We gotta murder these niggaz," E spat and curled his lip.

Wayne nodded. "Bitch-niggaz could've kilt my daughter. She say a bullet flew through the window and slammed two inches to the left of her head. Had she been sitting just slightly to the left, she would have been dead. I can't honor that shit. Let's make this happen. I gotta pick up a few shooters that's gon' rollout wit' us from the projects." He pulled away from the curb.

E pulled the AR-15 out of his coat and laid it across his lap. "Where that nigga Tez at?"

Wayne looked back at him before looking back at the road. "He at the Taylors in another van. We gon' rollout two vans deep and really hit up they temple. Hopefully we hit that nigga Caliph, too. I just got word from one of the li'l homies that fuck wit' the Stones that he the one put the hit on my cousin Zakir and gave the order for my crib to be shot up. He next in line to be prince over here in the Medina. They say he at the temple tonight, so I wanna go in there and make some noise. Y'all wit' me?" he asked, looking from me to E.

I slammed the clip into my Mach .90 and nodded. "I'm 'bout whatever you 'bout, li'l homie. Let's just handle this bitness and move on, you feel me?"

E smiled. "You ain't even gotta ask me. You already know what it is. Who is these shooters, though, that you snatching up?"

"The Vice Lords we just plugged up wit' to hustle out of the Taylors wanna prove they loyalty. They heard about what happened to my crib and wanna get down wit' us to show solidarity. They already know how them Stone niggaz get down. They say we gotta go at them hard right away or they gon' begin to holla at us real soon on some takeover-type shit. So, we gon' fuck wit' the Lords just to see how they get down."

I didn't know if I agreed wit' his plan to fuck wit' some niggaz we knew very little about, especially on a mission that involved us risking our lives. I knew from past experience the Black P. Stone mob wasn't nothin' to play wit'. They were all over Chicago and plugged with so many different gangs under the five-point star it was damn near suicide to even go at them. I felt like we should've handled bitness on our own, that way the Stones couldn't say for sure who came at them. By adding the Lords, it upped the chances that what took place tonight would be leaked to the enemy, and that in turn would cause us to be in a major bloody war. We didn't need that. But instead of me saying anything, I simply kept my mouth shut and rolled wit' the punches. Mentally, I was barely there because my every other thought was of Madison and the unread messages from Kenosha.

We met up wit' the Lords five minutes later, and I expected Tez to be there, but he wasn't. One of the Lords by the name of Vito came to the driver's side window of Wayne's van, reached his hand in, and they shook up. He was real skinny with long cornrows and a scar on the side of his face.

"I been in this temple over a hunnit times. Them fools gon' let me in. Once I get in, I'ma open the back door where they do their washing-up at before prayer. All y'all gotta do is come in through the back door and make them niggaz feel it. When they come running out the front, we gon' hit they ass up, too. Now, it's Friday, so majority of them in there. Caliph preaching a khutbah tonight. It's plenty of the brothas that come out just to hear him speak. Y'all handle y'all end, and we got ours. Let's cut the head off this snake before it slithers over to the Taylors and bite one of us."

Wayne nodded, and so did me and E, but as Vito was walking away from the van I hollered at him, "Say, Vito, where that nigga Tez at?"

He shrugged his shoulders. "I been hitting his phone, but he ain't answering. He told us what was what, and my niggaz on it."

At saying that, I saw about ten dudes run out of the Taylors with assault rifles in their hands and masks on their faces before they jumped in the Vice Lords' van.

As we were rolling off, I hit Tez's phone and sent him a text asking what was good, but I got no response.

***

Twenty minutes later I found myself ducked down next to Wayne at the back of the Black Stones' Temple. I could hear somebody preaching inside from the speakers. He was saying something about the lost tribe of Moab.

E came and put his back to the wall, then cocked his Uzi. "Wayne, I love you, nigga, and I love Wayneisha. I told you when she was born I would kill for her, and now I'm 'bout to show you. This loyalty is in blood, ma nigga, just like Racine always say." He leaned over and hugged Wayne, then pressed his back against the wall.

Wayne nodded. "Let's do this shit, bruh. I love both of you niggaz. It's Ski Mask until the death of me." He said this and made sure his mask was tight on his face by pulling it down and adjusting it. As soon as he said this, the back door to the Temple popped open, and we saw Vito waving us inside.

I jumped up with both Glock .40s in my hands, my eyes lowered into slits, and my heart beating faster than an African drummer on steroids, ready to handle my bitness. Wayne ran in front of me into the temple. I ran behind him with E behind me. The back door led into a bathroom-like facility. There were four dudes in there washing their feet in a basin.

Before I could even raise my gun, Wayne let loose with his Tech .9. *Bocka-bocka-bocka-bocka-bocka-bocka!* His bullets slammed into the dudes' faces and caused them to fall backward after their blood splashed against the bathroom walls.

I ran ahead of him and threw open the bathroom door, entering a hallway just as about ten dudes with kuffis on their heads tried to run toward the front door. I got to aiming for backs and heads. I wanted these niggaz dead.

Boom! Boom! Boom! Boom! Boom! Boom! Fire spit from my guns repeatedly, the bullets putting massive holes into their bodies before they fell to the ground, writhing in obvious pain. I felt nothin'. I hated these niggaz for damn-near killing Wayne's daughter. *Boom! Boom! Boom! Boom!* I spit constantly, letting my hammers sing.

Tat-tat-tat! Tat-tat-tat! Tat-tat-tat! "Fuck-niggaz!" E spit, chopping they ass down. I watched them shake while his bullets ripped into their bodies, then he ran ahead and into the Mosque, I guessed where the ceremony was taking place.

Before we got there, as soon as he opened the door, shots came in our direction. *Doom-doom-doom-doom! Boom! Boom! Boom! Boom!* The bullets came so fast I could barely react. I fell to my ass and scooted backward just as I felt my phone buzzing in my left front pocket.

Wayne let his Tech ride in their direction. *Bocka-bocka-bocka! Bocka-bocka-bocka-bocka-bocka! Click-click-click!* "Fuck, I'm out!" he said, turning and running toward the back door with me following him. I looked back to see E on one knee, letting his Uzi spit back at them. *Tat-tat-tat-tat-tat!* He jumped up and ran behind us.

Out of one of the hallways a door opened, and I saw a dude with a gauge about to put a hot one in my li'l homie. It was like it all happened in slow motion. I paused in my tracks, turned around, and waved for E to move out of the way. I saw his eyes get real big in his mask. He stopped and dropped to the floor, and as soon as he did, I let my pistols jump again and again before some fat nigga with dreads could get a shot off. *Boom! Boom! Boom! Boom! Boom! Boom! Boom!* The bullets stood him up before he fell to the ground. A pool of blood formed under him.

I ran to E and helped him up. "Come on, nigga!" We jumped up and followed Wayne through the back of the temple and out into the backyard. In the distance I could hear the Lords exchanging their gunfire at the temple, just like they said they would.

"Man, I love you, Racine! I love the fuck out of you, nigga! You saved my life! Fuck!" He hugged me with all his might as my phone buzzed again.

"Man, you good, bruh. Hold on, let me see who dis is." I broke the embrace wit' him and looked at my phone. It was a text from Kenosha saying meet her at our house ASAP! She said *Please respond, this is an emergency!*

I swallowed and told Wayne to storm to my crib out on Riverdale since we were no more than fifteen minutes away from there. The whole time all I could think about was Madison. I was panicking and once again imagining the worst happening to my daughter. I felt like I was getting ready to pass out.

"Say, look, Racine, we gon' drop you off and get rid of this van and all these weapons. Hit my phone in, like, three hours and tell me what's good. A'ight?" Wayne said as he pulled to the corner of my crib and let me out. I nodded, jumped out, and ran full-speed down the alley until I got to the back door of my place.

I took my key and let myself in real softly, creeping up the back steps and into the house. The first thing I saw that made me want to throw up was bloody footprints leading from my kitchen all the way through the house. "Kenosha! Kenosha! Baby, where are you?" I hollered with my pistol raised and leading the way. I got halfway through the house and saw her kneeling in front of a big, black Luis Vuitton suitcase with blood all over her.

She rocked back and forth on her knees, crying at the top of her lungs. "Why, Racine? Why?"

I ran into the living room and dropped down beside her, looking into the big suitcase that was overflowing with blood and limbs. My eyes grew bucked, and then my front door was kicked in.

Doom!

To Be Continued...
Ski Mask Cartel 4
Coming Soon

Submission Guideline.

Submit the first three chapters of your completed manuscript to ldpsubmissions@gmail.com, subject line: Your book's title. The manuscript must be in a .doc file and sent as an attachment. Document should be in Times New Roman, double spaced and in size 12 font. Also, provide your synopsis and full contact information. If sending multiple submissions, they must each be in a separate email.

Have a story but no way to send it electronically? You can still submit to LDP/Ca$h Presents. Send in the first three chapters, written or typed, of your completed manuscript to:

LDP: Submissions Dept
Po Box 870494
Mesquite, Tx 75187

DO NOT send original manuscript. Must be a duplicate.

Provide your synopsis and a cover letter containing your full contact information.

Thanks for considering LDP and Ca$h Presents.

T.J. EDWARDS

BOW DOWN TO MY GANGSTA

By **Ca$h**

TORN BETWEEN TWO

By **Coffee**

BLOOD STAINS OF A SHOTTA **III**

By **Jamaica**

WHEN THE STREETS CLAP BACK **III**

By **Jibril Williams**

STEADY MOBBIN

By **Marcellus Allen**

BLOOD OF A BOSS **V**

By **Askari**

LOYAL TO THE GAME **IV**

By **T.J. & Jelissa**

A DOPEBOY'S PRAYER **II**

By **Eddie "Wolf" Lee**

IF LOVING YOU IS WRONG… **III**

LOVE ME EVEN WHEN IT HURTS

By **Jelissa**

DAUGHTERS OF A SAVAGE **II**

By **Chris Green**

TRAPHOUSE KING **II**

By **Hood Rich**

BLAST FOR ME **II**

RAISED AS A GOON **V**

SKI MASK CARTEL 3

By **Ghost**

ADDICTIED TO THE DRAMA **III**

By **Jamila Mathis**

LIPSTICK KILLAH **III**

By **Mimi**

WHAT BAD BITCHES DO **II**

By **Aryanna**

THE COST OF LOYALTY **II**

By **Kweli**

SHE FELL IN LOVE WITH A REAL ONE

By **Tamara Butler**

LOVE SHOULDN'T HURT

By **Meesha**

CORRUPTED BY A GANGSTA **II**

By **Destiny Skai**

Available Now

RESTRAINING ORDER **I & II**

By **CA$H & Coffee**

LOVE KNOWS NO BOUNDARIES **I II & III**

By **Coffee**

RAISED AS A GOON I, II, III & IV

BRED BY THE SLUMS I, II, III

BLAST FOR ME

By **Ghost**

LAY IT DOWN **I & II**

LAST OF A DYING BREED

T.J. EDWARDS

BLOOD STAINS OF A SHOTTA I & II
By **Jamaica**
LOYAL TO THE GAME
LOYAL TO THE GAME II
LOYAL TO THE GAME III
By **TJ & Jelissa**
BLOODY COMMAS I & II
SKI MASK CARTEL I & II
By **T.J. Edwards**
IF LOVING HIM IS WRONG…I & II
By **Jelissa**
WHEN THE STREETS CLAP BACK I & II
By **Jibril Williams**
A DISTINGUISHED THUG STOLE MY HEART I II & III
By **Meesha**
PUSH IT TO THE LIMIT
By **Bre' Hayes**
BLOOD OF A BOSS **I, II, III & IV**
By **Askari**
THE STREETS BLEED MURDER **I, II & III**
THE HEART OF A GANGSTA I II& III
By **Jerry Jackson**
CUM FOR ME
CUM FOR ME 2
CUM FOR ME 3
An **LDP Erotica Collaboration**
BRIDE OF A HUSTLA **I II & II**

SKI MASK CARTEL 3

T.J. EDWARDS

THESE NIGGAS AIN'T LOYAL **I, II & III**
By **Nikki Tee**
GANGSTA SHYT **I II &III**
By **CATO**
THE ULTIMATE BETRAYAL
By **Phoenix**
BOSS'N UP **I , II & III**
By **Royal Nicole**
I LOVE YOU TO DEATH
By Destiny J
I RIDE FOR MY HITTA
I STILL RIDE FOR MY HITTA
By **Misty Holt**
LOVE & CHASIN' PAPER
By **Qay Crockett**
TO DIE IN VAIN
By **ASAD**
BROOKLYN HUSTLAZ
By **Boogsy Morina**
BROOKLYN ON LOCK I & II
By **Sonovia**
GANGSTA CITY
By **Teddy Duke**
A DRUG KING AND HIS DIAMOND I & II
A DOPEMAN'S RICHES
By Nicole Goosby
TRAPHOUSE KING

200

SKI MASK CARTEL 3

By **Hood Rich**
LIPSTICK KILLAH **I, II**
By **Mimi**

T.J. EDWARDS

BOOKS BY LDP'S CEO, CA$H

TRUST IN NO MAN

TRUST IN NO MAN 2

TRUST IN NO MAN 3

BONDED BY BLOOD

SHORTY GOT A THUG

THUGS CRY

THUGS CRY 2

THUGS CRY 3

TRUST NO BITCH

TRUST NO BITCH 2

TRUST NO BITCH 3

TIL MY CASKET DROPS

RESTRAINING ORDER

RESTRAINING ORDER 2

IN LOVE WITH A CONVICT

Coming Soon

BONDED BY BLOOD 2

BOW DOWN TO MY GANGSTA

SKI MASK CARTEL 3